"You're one brave lady."

"No." She shook her head. "I've never been so frightened in my life as I was this evening. I thought I'd lost them."

"The boys?"

"Yes."

Those dratted tears... Damn, they threatened to be her undoing. She blinked and sniffed and then blinked again.

"Good night, Matt. And...thank you."

And then, because she looked so rumpled and lost and forlorn, he couldn't help himself. He leaned forward and let his lips brush her forehead. "It was all my pleasure," he said softly. "Now stop thinking about the twins. Think only about yourself for a change. Sleep!"

PARENTS WANTED

Families in the making!

In the orphanage of a small Australian seaside town
called Bay Beach, there are little children desperately
in need of love. Some of them have no parents,
some are simply unwanted—but each child dreams
about having their own family someday....

The answer to their dreams can also be found in
Bay Beach! Couples who are destined for each other—
even if they don't know it yet—are brought together by love
for these tiny children. Can they find true love
themselves—and finally become a real family?

Look out in Harlequin Romance® in May
for the next PARENTS WANTED story:
The Doctors' Baby (#3702)
by
Marion Lennox

ADOPTED: TWINS!
Marion Lennox

PARENTS
WANTED

TORONTO • NEW YORK • LONDON
AMSTERDAM • PARIS • SYDNEY • HAMBURG
STOCKHOLM • ATHENS • TOKYO • MILAN • MADRID
PRAGUE • WARSAW • BUDAPEST • AUCKLAND

ISBN 0-373-03694-9

ADOPTED: TWINS!

First North American Publication 2002.

This edition published by arrangement with Harlequin Books S.A.

® and TM are trademarks of the publisher. Trademarks indicated with
® are registered in the United States Patent and Trademark Office, the
Canadian Trade Marks Office and in other countries.

Visit us at www.eHarlequin.com

Printed in U.S.A.

CHAPTER ONE

THE marital order in Bay Beach was thoroughly satisfactory for all concerned. Matt was marrying Charlotte. Erin, with her five unwanted children, was happily single.

Then the twins' bomb exploded.

Matt McKay was one of Australia's best known cattle breeders. He was also running late, but he wasn't so late that Charlotte would be annoyed. He'd been paying a visit to a friend in hospital. Now he was headed to Charlotte's for dinner.

He was also headed for commitment.

Well, why not? Charlotte was beautiful, immaculately groomed and extremely pleasant company. She understood his farming needs. Acclaimed as the best hostess in the district, she'd been loyal to Matt for almost twenty years.

Back in Bay Beach hospital, Matt's friend, Nick Daniels, was recovering nicely from his appendix operation. Matt had left him comfortably settled, Nick's wife and children pandering to his every whim.

The visit had made Matt think. Life should include pandering, he'd decided. He'd avoided it so far, but it was hard not to feel jealous of Nick's domestic bliss. Despite his lost appendix, Nick couldn't be more content.

Which was why Matt had detoured via the jewellers.

Something schmaltzy came onto the radio—something about love and snow-white hair and faithfulness forever.

Matt glanced down at the velvet box tucked into his map compartment, and he pushed away the last of his qualms. Marriage to Charlotte…

It had always seemed logical, and maybe that's why he'd taken so long to get around to asking. He'd had a few flings in his youth, but Charlotte was always calmly waiting for him to return from what she teasingly called his nonsense. Ten years ago her possessiveness had driven him nuts. But now… Maybe she was right. Maybe they were suited.

And he wouldn't mind a kid or two.

Nick was managing fatherhood beautifully, Matt decided, thinking of the family group he'd left at the hospital. With two gorgeous kids and another on the way, Nick and Shanni were blissfully happy.

Could he and Charlotte be the same?

Would Charlotte even want children? Charlotte wasn't a baby sort of person, but if she could produce little Charlottes… Children who were neat and practical and knew what was right…

That might be a problem. He wouldn't mind a bit of spirit in any child he had. He grinned to himself, acknowledging that he hadn't been a childhood angel. In fact he'd driven his mother to distraction.

But kids were a fifty-fifty gene split. He'd spent most of his childhood with his father, and if Charlotte thought she could breed children who'd wipe their feet and read their story books quietly, then maybe he could persuade her to give parenthood a try.

They could be hers indoors and his outdoors—which would be a childhood just like his had been.

So…

So tonight he'd finally ask her to marry him, he decided,

as he drove Charlotte-wards. After all, it was an excellent night.

Apart from a bomb waiting in the wings...

And at Home Number Three of Bay Beach Orphanage, things were also excellent.

Erin Douglas, Home Mother, had all her charges in bed by eight, which was no mean feat.

The baby, Marigold, had gone out like a light, bless her. She was showing every sign that she'd make her adoptive parents blissfully happy.

Five year old Tess and eight year old Michael, a brother and sister who'd been placed in the Home while their mother was ill, had gone to sleep on cue. No problems there.

And—amazingly—the twins had gone meekly to bed when told. When she'd checked ten minutes ago, they had their eyes closed and seemed out for the count.

This was truly amazing!

It was worth a glass of wine to celebrate, Erin decided. There weren't too many nights in a house mother's life when all her charges went to sleep this early, and it *never* happened when she had the twins.

Her hand stilled on the refrigerator door, survival instincts surfacing. It was almost too good to be true, she thought, and her well-honed nose smelled a rat. She tiptoed to the twins' bedroom yet again, and opened the door a crack.

But her instincts seemed wrong. They looked beautifully asleep.

How could she doubt them? she wondered as she gazed down at their intently sleeping countenances. How could anyone doubt them?

At seven years old, Henry and William were gorgeous. They had bright, curly, carrot-red hair, smatterings of freckles on their cute, snub noses, and a look on their faces that said they were the work of angels.

That look, Erin knew to her cost, was entirely misleading. There was a solid reason they were in care. Their mother couldn't control them, and by the time they were four, with no husband and seven other children to look after, she'd abused them unmercifully and then simply abandoned them to foster care.

That hadn't worked either. Up until now, no foster parents could cope with their trouble-making, and after each effort to find them a home, back they'd come to the orphanage every time. If it could be organised, they were placed with Erin. Erin could usually control them, but even Erin found it tough.

She sighed. What would she do with them? They were holy terrors, but as she looked down at their sleeping faces her heart twisted with pain for the two little boys she was starting to love.

They shouldn't be in the orphanage. They were sharp as tacks—maybe clever enough to be categorised as intellectually gifted, Erin thought, remembering a few of the truly amazing spots of trouble they'd landed themselves into. As well as that, they were engaging and lovable, and they desperately needed a mother and a father to love them.

If only they weren't intent on destroying the world!

Still, for now they were asleep and she was feeling as if a miracle had occurred! She took herself back to the kitchen, kicked off her shoes and put her feet up in bliss.

'Here's to a miracle,' she told herself, raising her wine glass in a toast to the evening. 'Here's to an excellent night.'

*   *   *

Back in their bedroom, Henry and William's plan was working like a dream.

They'd strung thread from the kitchen door to the top of their bedroom door. Then they'd tied their stuffed toy, Tigger Tiger, to the thread, and they'd frayed it so it'd break at the first movement of the kitchen door.

The plan was perfect. If Erin left the kitchen, the thread snapped and Tigger fell to the floor. Unless the thread tangled in Erin's feet—which would have been really, really unlucky—she'd never notice.

As Tigger landed, there was just enough time for the boys to shove what they were doing under the bed, grab Tigger, scramble under the bedcovers and flick off the light before Erin appeared to check.

So to Erin, all was beautifully, unnaturally normal, and they concentrated fiercely on looking asleep as she tiptoed over to them.

'Goodnight, you rascals,' she'd whispered, and they'd both had to concentrate even harder not to giggle.

Then, with Erin gone, they picked up the end of the thread and retied Tigger in his warning position. And then they retrieved what was under the bed.

Brilliant! Absolutely excellent.

But the bomb wasn't meant to go off when it did.

The plan was for Henry to carry it outside in the toe of his slipper. It was scary to carry it in his bare fingers, and a slipper should hold it safe. Their bomb was a hand-taped ball stuffed with matches and fire-crackers, designed to go off when thumped on the ground. They knew how volatile it was, but they weren't stupid.

After carrying it carefully outside, the plan was to lob it over the next-door fence.

It was eight at night. At eight *every night*, just as the

news ended on the telly, their next door neighbours, Helmut and Valda Cole, let their pet poodle out for her evening run.

Pansy Poodle never went more than two feet into the garden so there was no fear of hitting her. But she might just about turn inside out with the bang, and Mr and Mrs Cole would go berserk. Which would be very interesting indeed!

Henry and William disliked the Coles, and they knew exactly what the Coles thought about them—and orphans in general. The Coles were raising a petition to have all the orphanage houses put together. 'To put all the trouble-makers in the one spot!' They were even nasty to Erin, which was unthinkable.

Henry and William mightn't always do as Erin wanted, but she gave the best cuddles of anyone they knew, and even when they were in serious trouble she just sighed, ruffled their hair and said, 'What am I going to do with you, you twerps?'

And Pansy Poodle yapped so much she woke the baby, and when Henry poked his finger through the fence—just to say hello—she'd bitten him! It had taken fifteen minutes of Erin's cuddles before Henry had stopped shaking.

The Coles, therefore, had to be got rid of before they upset Erin further, or before Pansy bit someone else, and the only thing that might make them move was if they thought their poodle was in danger. Hence the bomb, the construction of which had been learned from spying on the bigger kids at school.

Only then...

Well, Henry was pushing the bomb into the slipper and William was holding the slipper up so it'd slide in, and it wouldn't quite fit—and then Henry got nervous and the slipper sort of fell sideways.

The tape-wound ball, stacked really, really tightly with matches and firecrackers, fell heavily onto the floor and rolled under the curtains by the bed.

Henry and William stared at it for one horrified moment—and then dived for cover under the opposite bed.

The explosion reverberated through the house and into the night beyond. Instantly the lights went off as the electricity safety switch cut in, and there was the sound of crashing glass from along the veranda. The smell of smoke swept into the kitchen, and then the fire alarm in the corridor ceiling started to scream.

Bay Beach Orphanage, Home Number Three, was on fire.

Matt heard the fire alarm before he rounded the corner. That was no big deal, he thought. His smoke detector at home went off every time he burned his toast. Which, he had to admit, was often.

But Matt was driving with his truck window down, and the alarm was loud enough to make him glance sideways. He was now right out front of one of the Bay Beach Homes—and what he saw made him slam his foot on the brake and pull to dead halt.

He left his truck sitting where it was, engine still on, and he started to run.

'Take the baby.'

Matt knew Erin Douglas. Of course he did. Everyone in Bay Beach knew everyone else, and these two had gone to school together.

Not that they'd got on. Erin was three years younger than Matt, and maybe he still thought of her as the bossy, forthright kid she'd been way back in third grade. Over the years he'd danced with her a few times at local functions, but she definitely wasn't his type.

It didn't stop him appreciating her. With a lovely figure; with a clear, almost luminescent complexion and huge blue eyes, she'd always had her share of boyfriends. She was definitely attractive, he'd decided, in a blonde, curvy sort of way, but she was a bit...well, sassy, and inclined to laugh at the world—and at him in particular.

Matt was wealthy and his family were descended from the landed gentry. Normally that stood him in good stead with women, but with Erin it was almost as if she was mocking him because of it.

And she always looked frazzled, he thought. She didn't fuss if her shoulder-length curls were tangled, and her make-up was always scant and looked like it had been applied in haste. Yeah, he knew all the Home Mothers looked like that—they had such little time to themselves—but it wouldn't hurt her to take a bit more effort.

She wore brightly coloured dresses, nipped in to a neat waistline and then blousing out in soft folds to mid-calf. They looked home-made, Charlotte had told him, and he could see that they were.

The last time he'd seen her had been at the local school fête. One of her kids had painted her face as a butterfly, and her blue eyes were orbs under enormous, colourful wings, the paint reaching right out to her ears.

Good grief, he'd thought, as he and Charlotte had paused for a second, stunned look. No, she definitely wasn't his type. She wasn't groomed and elegant as he liked his women. She wasn't like his mother or like Charlotte.

And now... Well, she certainly wasn't concentrating on appearances, but she was looking more frazzled than he'd ever seen her. As he reached the veranda, she burst through the screen door and she was carrying a baby. The little one couldn't have been more than four or five months old.

Erin didn't say anything more than, 'Take the baby,' before thrusting the child into his arms and disappearing again into the house.

What was he supposed to do with it? He stared down at the baby in indecision. He couldn't just dump it, but there were things that were more urgent here than baby-holding.

A face appeared over the side fence. Well, it would. The explosion must have been heard for blocks, and Valda Cole was into everyone else's business before it happened. Usually Matt avoided Valda like the plague, but now, burdened with the baby, he was even grateful to see her.

'Take the baby and phone the fire brigade,' he snapped, and thrust the infant over the fence into her startled arms before she had a chance to protest. 'And contact the police and ambulance. Fast.'

And then he dived into the house after Erin.

She'd found Tess and Michael.

The children had woken and stumbled to their doors in the increasingly smoke-filled dark. Calling and feeling her way, she found them and grabbed their hands. Five years old and badly frightened, Tess stumbled in the gloom. Still holding eight-year-old Michael's hand, Erin lifted Tess and fumbled her way out toward the door.

The smoke was so thick she couldn't see anything. Her eyes were streaming as she called to the twins.

'Henry? William?'

There was no answer. Ventilation slits were built in above the bedroom doors and the smoke seemed to be coming from the twins' room, but she couldn't investigate. Her first priority must be to get Tess and Michael out.

And then she barrelled right into Matt in the hall.

This time she acknowledged his presence. She needed help—any help!—and she knew enough of Matthew McKay to know he was capable.

'Matt, there's these two, but the twins are still inside.' She propelled her children forward and choked on a lungful of smoke. 'Take them out.'

He took them all out. Grasping her arm without a word, he pulled her back out of the door before she could argue. There, standing on the porch, she fought to regain her breath so she could speak again.

Her panic was threatening to overwhelm her. The smoke seemed almost impenetrable, and she could see flames shooting from the side window. It was definitely coming from the twins' room.

'Dear God, the twins...' It was hard to make her voice work. The smoke had seared her lungs, so every breath hurt.

'How many more are inside?' Matt's voice was harsh with authority. 'How many and tell me where they are. Now!'

Somehow she hauled herself under control and made herself heard. She couldn't have asked for a better assistant than Matt McKay. Sure, he was wealthy and too good-looking for his own good, and he moved in circles she didn't belong too, but his competence was never in question.

'Just the twins,' she told him. 'Two seven-year-old boys. They're in there together.' She choked on another lungful of smoke, but she had enough sense to thrust the children off the porch as she motioned toward the twins' window. The curtains were billowing out through the smashed glass, flaming outward in the night air. 'Please look after the kids. I'll go—'

'Stay where you are!' Matt's brain was in overdrive as he sorted priorities. Helmut Cole was running across the lawn with a garden hose, while Valda watched horrified from a distance. She was holding the baby like she was holding something unclean.

It couldn't matter. At least the baby could come to no harm where she was, and Helmut was doing the right thing.

'Have you called emergency services?' he yelled and, as Valda nodded, he turned back to her husband.

'Helmut, point the hose in that window and keep it there.' Then he turned and headed back inside—back in the direction of those shooting flames.

'Please be careful.' Erin was close to collapse. 'The smoke…'

'We can't get in through the window,' he told her. 'Let's just hope the whole bedroom isn't ablaze.'

The house was in pitch darkness, but even if it had been daylight he couldn't have seen anything. The smoke was so dense it was threatening to choke him. Matt dropped to his knees and crawled, but the smoke was too thick…

Then his brain kicked in. Finally! Damn, he should have thought of this outside. He paused, hauled off his sweater and tied it round his face. It wasn't much protection, but it was better than nothing.

The twins' bedroom was the second window from the front. He needed to turn right through the kitchen and head for the second door along the passage to the closed door…

He had to work fast, whatever was behind that door. If he was met with a wall of flame he didn't have a chance— but then, neither did the twins.

With a silent prayer, he felt the knob, but it wasn't hot to touch. That was his first good sign. There was therefore only smoke hard against the door. There was nothing to do now but...

He took a deep, smoke-filled breath, opened the door and forced his eyes to see. The curtains across the window were blazing, and the bed against the far wall was well alight. Outside, Helmut raised his hose and he was hit in the face by a jet of water.

Thank God for Helmut. The water wouldn't put the fire out, but it helped keep him alive. The soggy sweater across his face made breathing possible—just—and he kept his face in that direction until the sweater was completely soaked.

Then he took another breath and somehow managed to make his voice work.

'Kids, where are you?'

'H-here...' The muffled gasp came from the side of the room away from the window—low down. A piece of burning curtain landed in his hair. He thrust it away, unconscious of the pain, and groped under the second bed.

'Grab hold,' he managed, and small hands reached out and gripped his arms. As he counted contact hands—four!—he could have sobbed in relief.

There was no time for sobbing. Now what? Somehow he had to get them back through the house, and the smoke was building every minute.

'T-Tigger,' one of the children was saying, and the kid was pulling away.

'What?'

'Tigger.'

Matt found his hands full of sodden fur as the thing was thrust at him. A toy? Good grief! He shoved it down his shirt and grabbed a blanket.

'Wait.' His voice came out as a hoarse croak. More of Helmut's water hit the blanket, but not enough. He held it up and let it soak, and then threw the cloth over the boys' heads.

'We're crawling out of the room,' he croaked. He had them cradled against him, but he pushed them towards the door. 'You crawl first. If I stop, then you keep going. That's an order. Now!'

And he shoved them forward out of that burning room, along the passage, into the kitchen and the hall beyond.

'Henry... William...'

Erin met them in the hall. Like Matt, she'd wrapped her sweater over her head. She'd come in as far as she dared and was waiting, crouched at the kitchen door. As they crawled from the passage, she hauled them into her arms and tugged them outside.

Matt followed. He crawled four feet from the front door and collapsed unconscious onto the porch.

The most beautiful pair of blue eyes was gazing down into his.

'Do you think he'll live?'

There was something over his mouth and nose—something plastic and hard, and he tried to push it away.

'Keep it there, Matt.' He recognised the voice—Rob McDonald, the local police sergeant. 'You've got a lungful of smoke and we're giving you oxygen. Yes, Erin, if he's capable of fighting off a mask, then I reckon he'll live.'

Matt thought that through, and it seemed to make sense. The gorgeous eyes were still looking at him. It was funny how he'd never noticed them before. Erin was grimy and smoke-stained and still looking frazzled, but suddenly he thought she looked the most beautiful woman he'd ever seen. Just like that butterfly at the fête, he thought dazedly. Gorgeous!

Life was gorgeous!

If she hadn't come in to find them, he never would have got the boys out, he acknowledged. It had taken all his strength just to crawl those last few yards and he couldn't have propelled the twins any further.

'The twins?' It was a muffled whisper under the mask, but Erin knew what he was saying.

'They're scared out of their wits but they're fine. I need to go back to them. If you're sure you're okay...'

'He's tough,' Rob growled. 'The ambulance boys are just bringing the stretcher across.'

That roused him. Hell, no. He didn't need a stretcher. He pushed the mask away, coughed and coughed again, and finally managed to sit up. Rob stayed by his side, uneasy.

'They told me to hold the mask over your face. Do you mind not getting me into trouble?'

'I don't need it.' Matt coughed again, grabbed the mask and took two deep breaths to prove it. The improvement was immediate.

Then he took a look around, and was astounded by what he saw.

People were everywhere. The fire engine was parked almost beside him; there were men running, hoses uncoiling; the police car was there with its blue light flashing...

Half of Bay Beach was here, he thought dazedly, and then he turned to the house.

Helmut's hose hadn't been enough. The house was well alight and they'd be lucky to save anything. The bedroom where the twins had come from was now a charred shell, and the rest of the house was roofless and smouldering. There was little for the fire-fighters to do but to play their hoses over the ruin to stop sparks causing trouble elsewhere.

Matt looked at the charred remains of the twins' bedroom, and a shudder ran though his entire body. He'd been in there. The twins had been in there!

The man beside him saw what he was seeing and guessed his thoughts. 'You got the kids out,' Rob said in a voice that was none too steady. His big policeman's hand came down and grasped Matt's shoulder. 'I don't know how you did it, mate, but you did. You're a bloody hero.'

'I don't know how I did it either,' Matt said. He gulped in two more takes of oxygen and focussed some more.

There was something heavy and soggy in his shirt and he suddenly remembered the kids' toy. Or whatever it was. He peered down his shirt in the combined firelight and floodlights, and was relieved to see a pair of grimy glass eyes staring up at him.

It *was* just a toy, then. Great! For a minute there he'd thought maybe it was an unconscious pet, and mouth-to-mouth resuscitation on a dog or cat didn't really appeal.

Back to important stuff.

'The kids…they really are okay?'

'They really are okay. Thanks to you.' Rob looked up as the ambulance officers approached and he gave them an apologetic grin. 'He's giving me trouble.'

'He would.' The ambulance officers were locals and they were mates of both Rob and Matt. Their smiles were wide as houses.

In truth as they'd rounded the bend and seen the fire their stomachs had tightened in horror. Fire casualties were awful, and kids were the worst. Now, they were having trouble containing their delight that their only patient was a stroppy mate—a mate who looked like he had every intention of making it to old age.

'Let's get you loaded up and off to hospital,' they said cheerfully. 'Hey, we hear Nick Daniels is in there without his appendix. You can keep him company.'

'I'm not going to hospital.'

'Too right you are, even if we have to tie you down.' Then they glanced up as a young woman came hurrying across the lawn toward them, her doctor's bag at her side. 'Doc, he's saying he won't come to hospital.'

'Lie down, Matthew McKay,' she said firmly.

'But—'

'Shut up and let me examine you or I'll put you out for the count.' Dr Emily Mainwaring knew her stuff, and she knew her patient. 'Hurry up, Matt. They say you're the one worst affected but I have five kids and Erin to examine, so let's get this over fast.'

He was fine. Excellent, almost.

'You'll live,' she told him, tucking away her stethoscope and casting a brief yet horrified glance at the still-smouldering house. 'Just don't push your luck any further. You need antiseptic and a dressing on that burn on your head, but it's superficial.' Then she peered closer under his shirt and saw what he'd stuffed there. 'What on earth is that?'

'It's a toy of some kind.' Matt managed a grin. 'It's not a patient—thank Heaven.' He put a hand down to haul it out but she stopped him.

'No. If it really is a toy, leave it there and see if you can clean it up when you get home. If you leave it here it'll get lost in this mess, and it just may be important. These kids have lost everything, and I suspect I'm not looking at long-term physical problems here, but psychological ones.'

He thought that through and it made sense. 'Okay.' The toy could stay, soggy or not.

'Can you dress that burn yourself? It's not too bad.' She was flustered, worrying about Erin and the kids and wanting to move on. 'Good. Okay, you don't need hospital, but

I do want you supervised tonight. No going home to that farm alone. What about going to Charlotte's? Shall I have someone ring her?'

'No!' For some reason that was the last thing he wanted. 'I'm fine.'

'You hear what I'm saying?' she said fiercely. 'Home with someone with you—or hospital. Choose.'

'I...'

'I don't have time to waste,' she said firmly. 'Think about it while I check the rest. Though, thanks to you, I gather I hardly have a patient to contend with.' She turned to the ambulance officers.

'Hold him down, boys, and don't let him go until he can give me a plan for this evening that doesn't involve going home by himself, forgetting the antiseptic, having three stiff whiskies and passing out without anyone there to watch.'

She meant it.

Matt knew Emily well enough to accept that she was quite capable of trussing him to a stretcher, and he had enough wit—and he was feeling bad enough—to acknowledge that she was talking sense.

So what were his alternatives?

She'd suggested Charlotte's, but the idea was distinctly unappealing. Sure, she'd put him up for the night, but she'd fuss.

All he wanted was his own bed, he thought, and suddenly he wanted it very, very much. Shock was starting to hit home, and he had to clench his hands into fists to stop Rob seeing the sudden tremor that ran through him.

But Rob wasn't noticing. His mind had moved on.

'What can we do with the kids?' The police sergeant was still beside Matt, but he was speaking to Erin. The doctor and the ambulance officers were attending the children.

With immediate health fears eased, it was time to concentrate on the next problem, which seemed, Matt gathered, to be accommodation for Erin and the children.

Erin was tightening her lips, thinking it through. Or, she was trying to think it through. She looked like her mind felt full of smoke.

'I don't know,' she managed, and then she looked up as someone else darted through the jumble of fire-hoses and fire-fighters. Her strained face slackened in relief. 'Wendy...'

Wendy was an ex-House Mother, now happily married and immersed in domesticity. She was followed by her husband, Luke. Luke strolled languidly through the chaos, lifted a trembling Michael into his arms almost as an aside—marriage to Wendy meant that Luke and the Orphanage kids had met each other heaps of times before—and he hugged the little boy close.

'Hey, Michael. Been having some excitement, then? Wow! It's great that you're all okay. And this is a great fire engine.'

Then he looked down at Matt in admiring amusement. 'And here's our Matthew out for the count. Been playing heroes, have we, kids?'

'Shut up, Luke.' But Matt grinned. It suddenly did feel good. Heroic even. The feel of those four little hands clutching his arms from under the bed came sweeping back, and he knew where they'd be now without him...

His grin faded and the tremors swept back. He'd been lucky to get them—and himself—out alive.

'The other homes are all full,' Wendy was saying. She was right back in House Mother mode, as though she'd never left. She was hugging Michael's little sister, Tess, to her breast as if she was her own. 'Erin, Shanni was at the hospital with Nick when the call came through. The nurse in charge told her what was going on, so she rang us first thing. I rang Lori on Luke's cell phone on the way here. Lori's on her way, but we need to sort the kids out.'

'Yes.' That made it through Erin's fog. Lori was House Mother at Home Number Five, and the only one without tiny tots to care for. They'd need her, but Erin was in no state to concentrate.

Wendy recognised it. She came forward and gave her friend a hug like her husband was giving Michael, then she kept right on holding her, Tess somehow squashed in the middle. Which Tess didn't seem to mind at all. 'Hey, kid, you and Matt got them all out,' she told her friend. 'Everyone's safe. You did good.'

'The twins…they must have been making something.' Erin was trembling in her friend's arms, and, from where he was lying on the ground, Matt had an almost unbearable urge to rise and take over. He wanted to hug her as well.

Which was crazy. He grabbed the oxygen mask and took two more deep breaths. He wasn't himself here.

'I've been thinking,' Wendy said into her friend's hair. 'Tess and Michael are only with you until their mother gets out of hospital at the week-end. Luke and I talked about it as we drove here and we can take them until then. They know us.'

Tess and Michael's mother was on her own, and she was a severe asthmatic. She was in and out of hospital often, and Tess and Michael were frequent visitors to the Homes. They'd be happy with Wendy, Erin knew. But…

'That still leaves Marigold and the twins.'

'Tess and Michael will be shocked,' Wendy said gently, gathering Tess closer as she spoke. The doctor was checking the twins, and the little girl was starting to tremble. 'They'll need lots of care, so I don't think Luke and I can do much more than take them. I talked to Lori and she said the same. She's thinking about the baby and the twins now. And speaking of Lori…'

Lori arrived then. Thirtyish and competent—as all the house mothers were—she might be shocked, but she took right over where Wendy left off.

'It's fine for Michael and Tess to go with Wendy,' she said directly. 'It makes sense. But the other Homes are packed. Maybe we can use the hotel as an interim measure.'

'Erin can't look after Marigold tonight,' Wendy told her. 'Look at her. She's shocked to the core. The last thing she needs is two o'clock feeds. She needs to sleep. And the twins—'

'No one but Erin can control the twins,' Lori said bluntly.

'Yeah, look at how I controlled them,' Erin retorted. 'That's control?' She gestured to where the flames were dying and leaving a charred and smoking ruin, and she shuddered.

'And the publican's heard of the twins,' Lori added. 'I guess we might have trouble persuading him to take you.'

'You bet we'll have trouble.'

'But the baby's up for adoption and her placement's due on Monday,' Lori said, brightening. 'I guess I could squeeze Marigold in with me until then. She's such a great baby.' She glanced around to where Valda was holding her at arm's length, a look of complete disgust on her face. The baby, it seemed, had started to smell.

They all knew it didn't matter. Lori had decreed Marigold was a great baby, and so had her prospective parents. She'd survive a few more minutes of Valda's disgust. 'That just leaves Erin and the twins.'

'I don't know about the hotel,' Erin said doubtfully. 'Maybe we could stay with Shanni.'

'Shanni has two kids, is pregnant and has a sick husband.' Wendy was suddenly in charge again. 'And I can't take any more than Michael and Tess.' Then she looked down at Matt and her brow grew thoughtful. 'Hmm.'

Hmm?

Matt gazed upward and he didn't like the way Wendy was looking at him.

Wendy, Erin, Shanni, Lori... Even Doc Emily. They were all the same. They were organising, bossy women, in a sensible, non-Charlotte type of way that you couldn't just ignore by going outside and heaving a few hay bales until it was time for dinner.

Frankly, they scared him to death.

He took two more breaths of oxygen from his mask and tried to look pathetic. It didn't come off. In fact, it seemed to make things worse.

'Doc says you're not to go home alone, and I know you live in that great rambling place all by yourself.' Wendy was onto her good idea like a hound on a scent and she wasn't to be distracted. 'What could be more appropriate than Erin and the twins coming home with you to keep you company?'

'*The twins?*' He'd seen enough of the twins!

'You saved their lives,' Wendy said, her voice softening, as she crouched beside him. Her eyes met his. They were inches apart and he couldn't argue if he wanted to. 'And maybe you saved Erin's, too, as I know she'd have tried to get them out herself if it wasn't for you. So you can't just turf them out on the street, now can you?'

'I...' It was too much. 'No,' he said weakly. 'I suppose I can't.'

'So you can have them?'

He forced himself to think. He wouldn't make much of a host. 'I need to be away occasionally, for cattle shows and things...'

'But they can look after themselves with ease. So that's that,' Wendy said triumphantly, and she rose and hugged Erin harder. 'It's all sorted, my love, so you can stop shaking this very minute. All of you. Drama over. All we have is one burned house to rebuild and we'll be back to normal. Now as soon as the doctor's cleared the lot of you then you can go out to Matt's. I can see the Welfare Shop lady over by the fire chief. Good old Edna. She's always armed with a stockpile of emergency clothes. I'll see how she can help and then we'll send you all home. Together.'

CHAPTER TWO

FOR how long?

All we have is one burned house to rebuild and we'll be back to normal.

It occurred to Matt as they started out to the farm that this might be no short undertaking. The Bay Beach Home lay in ruins, and finding accommodation in this town was next to impossible. Rented houses were taken by tourists at big dollars, and everything else...

Everything else would have to wait. 'Worry about to-morrow tomorrow,' he told himself, glancing back at the cavalcade behind him. Rob was driving him home in Matt's truck—'because there's no way you're driving to-night,' the doctor had decreed, and Matt could only agree. He didn't even feel like driving.

Behind them was the police car, driven by a police constable and containing Erin and the twins. Behind that another helper was driving Erin's Home car. That car held enough Welfare donations to clothe a small republic.

Heck!

He glanced back again and Erin was sitting in the passenger seat of the car behind. They were just turning out of town, and as they passed under a street lamp she looked right back at him, raised her eyebrows and gave him a quizzical look that said she knew exactly what he was thinking.

That this was a disaster.

This was just great!

He had a mind-reading, bossy tenant, with twins and

trouble attached. His nice bachelor existence looked like it was being threatened in a much more dire way than when he'd thought earlier that he might—just *might*, mind you, definitely not *would*—ask Charlotte to marry him.

Charlotte was one thing. Married to Charlotte, he knew he'd be free to carry on with life as normal, and his emotional involvement would be minimal.

But life with Erin and twins?

Life could just be chaos.

Then he twisted back to face the road ahead as Rob applied the brakes. Behind them, the cavalcade slowed as well.

'I think this might be someone wanting to speak to you,' Rob said, and he gave him the same quizzical look that he'd just received from Erin. 'If I'm not mistaken, it's your Charlotte.'

His Charlotte…

Once more he had that sensation of entrapment—the sensation he'd had since he was about thirteen and Charlotte had told the district he was the man she intended marrying. Of course it was Charlotte, driving her smart little red BMW and pulling to a halt as Rob steered Matt's truck to a halt on the grass verge. Then she was out of the car and darting across the road toward them.

Charlotte was looking immaculate. Of course. When had she not? She was wearing her signature, beautifully cut, white slacks and white silk blouse, her long, blonde hair was carefully braided into a chignon, and she looked all ready for their intimate dinner.

Except she was no longer expecting her special dinner. Bay Beach had a very effective communication system, and it hadn't let Charlotte down. She'd heard of the fire. Hauling the truck door open before Matt could do it himself, she practically threw herself into his arms in relief.

'Matthew... Oh, love, you could have been killed.' But emotion or not, her eyes were taking everything in, including Rob—and including the red velvet box lying forgotten in the map compartment. Sensibly, she ignored it. Almost.

'Sally rang and she said you dived into that burning building and pulled out the orphans all by yourself. She said you were burned!' She stepped back and saw the nasty red blister on his forehead and the grime of smoke all over him—and then, instinctively, she looked down at herself.

Whoops. Her pure white ensemble was now smudged grey.

House fires, however, required courage. Matt had been brave and she could be, too.

'It'll wash off,' she told her beloved. 'Not to worry. But, Matt, Sally said the doctor said you're not to stay alone.' She turned to Rob. 'Bring him to my place.'

It was time Matt put a word in, but it was tricky to do. However, Rob was made of sterner stuff.

'We can't,' Rob said, and thumbed back to the cavalcade. 'Matt's got all the company he needs.'

Charlotte looked back—and then stared in horror as she saw who was in the police car. 'Not the orphans!' she gasped. 'You're not taking the orphans home with you. Matt, you're burned!'

'I can cope.'

'You can't.'

'Charlotte, there's only two kids needing a place to stay, and Erin will take care of them.' Matt was growing uneasy now. Erin had emerged from the police car and was walking over to see what was happening. From where she was now, she could hear every word Charlotte said. 'Erin's been through a lot, Charlotte.'

'I'm sure she has.' Charlotte shook her head in disbelief

that this could be happening. 'But darling, so have you.'
She turned her head and raised her voice. 'Erin, Matt's
coming back to my house. He needs to be looked after.
Your organisation can look after you.'

Whoa…

Erin took a deep breath. Count to ten, she told herself.
This is important.

Charlotte was *not* one of Erin's favorite people. Lovely
and gracious, and generous to people she considered the
'right sort', her graciousness had never extended to Erin.
Erin was three years younger and about a million miles
below her on the social ladder. As she'd grown older,
Charlotte had grown more adept at hiding her distaste for
those she considered beneath her, but somehow Erin always knew exactly where she stood. Right on the bottom
rung!

But, like Charlotte, Erin could be ruthless when she
needed to be, and she needed to be ruthless now.
'Charlotte, Matt's offered us accommodation.'

'I don't care if he has.' Up until now, Charlotte had had
a wonderful feeling about this evening. The sight of that
tiny crimson box confirmed she'd been right, and now all
it had come to was *this*! 'Anyone can see he's unwell.'

And so was Erin. She'd been through enough without
Charlotte's arguments. Back in the police car were two
subdued little boys who needed a bed, fast. She knew well
enough that at Matt's house she would find one—and one
for herself, too.

There wasn't an alternative.

'Matt's offered to take us in and I've accepted,' she said,
and there was a certain amount of grit in her voice. 'I'm
sorry, Charlotte, but we've been through too much tonight
to stand on the road and argue. If you could just let us
go…'

'Matt's hurt.'

'Then follow him home and fix him up,' Erin replied wearily. 'I'm sure I can't do it with your style. A sticking plaster and a push in the direction of bed is all I'm capable of, believe me.'

Charlotte glared. She didn't like this one bit.

But what was the alternative? Charlotte was thinking on her feet, and she was thinking fast.

Firstly—naturally—she was thinking that Erin was attractive and unmarried and she didn't like the thought of such a woman staying with Matt. But then, Matt had known Erin for ages—since childhood in fact—and he hadn't seemed attracted in the past. So maybe that was okay.

Her eyes moved imperceptibly sideways. He'd already purchased the contents of the box, so she needed to concentrate on priorities.

Which were, secondly, that Erin was saddled with the twins. They might be subdued now but the whole town knew their reputation. Matt would be driven crazy before he could get used to them in the house.

The only alternative open to her now was to invite them all back to her place, and that didn't bear thinking of. She had a perfect little horse stud in the hills; the house was immaculate and children would destroy it.

What else then? Create a scene? No! She knew Matt would hate it. She'd worked so hard to make him see her as the perfect wife that she'd be a fool to mess it up now.

The velvet box was there, like a tantalising promise. She could concede a little.

'Okay, sweetheart,' she said softly, ignoring Erin totally and turning back to her intended. 'You go ahead. I'll bring your dinner over.'

'My dinner?' Matt was still too befuddled to think.

'You were coming to my place for dinner. Quails with the most gorgeous sauce... I've kept it hot for you.' She gave him her most loving look, and he responded with gratitude. But he didn't want her quails.

'Eggs on toast is all I'm capable of tonight,' he said wearily. 'I'm sorry, Charlotte. Freeze my dinner. It'll have to wait for some other time.'

This wasn't going to work.

Erin had never been inside Matt's house, but she walked through the front door and she darn near walked out again. This and the twins? No and no and no.

'You'd best take off your shoes,' Matt said, through force of habit. 'The carpet shows every mark.'

'I'd guess it would.' Erin stared at the floor in doubt, but obligingly removed her shoes and then turned to the boys and slipped theirs off too.

The twins let her do what she wanted and they hardly moved as she did. The Welfare lady had dressed them—sort of—but they were so subdued they hadn't said a word. Now Erin badly wanted to get them alone. She wanted them bathed and tucked up somewhere warm and safe and alone, where she could cuddle the shock and fear out of them.

Matt was stooping to help with their shoes, and she was grateful for that at least.

'Did...did you choose this carpet—or did Charlotte?' she managed. It was a stupid conversation starter, but it was something.

'My mother chose it,' he said stiffly and that made her blink in surprise, memories flooding back.

She'd known Matt's mother—not that they'd ever spoken, of course. Matt's family owned one of the wealthiest farms in the district. Not so Erin's. As one of eight kids in a big, loving and decidedly impoverished family, Erin was considered by Mrs McKay to be a nobody.

Which suited her nicely, she acknowledged. Erin had no wish to move in Matt and Charlotte's exclusive world. She and her friends—and their respective parents—used to check out Louise McKay's perfectly tailored white suits and think how impractical they were. Only Louise thought they were perfect.

'Didn't your mother die five years ago?' Erin managed, thrusting away memories of the perfect Louise. 'This carpet looks unused.'

'I usually use the back door,' he told her. Then he managed a grin. 'I guess Mum trained me well—or I got sick of taking off my boots.'

'I can see that.' She stared at the white carpet, and then through to the white leather lounge suite in the sitting room beyond. 'The boys and I had better get used to the back door as well.'

'I guess it'd be best.'

Hmm.

The situation here was decidedly strained. Erin was standing in the front hall of the great McKay family home. Alone—apart from the twins—with Matt McKay. The feeling was...weird?

But she didn't have the time to examine her personal feelings. The boys' needs were too great. 'Show me the bathroom and where the boys can sleep,' she said wearily. 'They need to be in bed.'

So did Matt. He gave himself a mental shake, trying to sort priorities. There were two bathrooms. He could clean up in one while she coped with the twins in the other. Maybe he could help her, but first he had to clear his head. It still felt fogged with smoke and the aftermath of terror.

'This way.' He led them, minus their shoes, to the back of the house. Here were two bedrooms side by side, with a bathroom between. To Erin's delight, the beds were freshly made, as if he'd been expecting guests any day.

'It's another legacy from my mother,' he told her, seeing her look of surprise. 'The bedrooms stay immaculate at all times in case of unexpected visitors. That's you. Unexpected visitors.' He managed another of his smiles, and even though it was crooked and weary it was a smile that made a girl want to take a backward step.

Or a forward step?

But he was talking in a dragging voice that had Erin suddenly looking sharply up at him. She needed to focus here. The burn on his forehead was blistering badly and his eyes were red-rimmed from the smoke. He might be hero material but he was badly shocked and he'd inhaled a lot more smoke than she had.

'I'm afraid they won't stay immaculate if my twins are sleeping in them,' she said apologetically, and then, propelling her charges into the bathroom, she turned back to him with decision written all over her. House mother personified. 'You go and take a shower yourself,' she said. 'And then go straight to bed.'

'We'll see. I do need to eat. I'll meet you in the kitchen when the twins are settled.' He managed a rueful smile. 'That is, if you dare leave them alone.'

'They'll be good tonight,' Erin told him, and she smiled as she ruffled the twins' soot-blackened hair. The children were so tired they were sagging on their feet. 'Won't you, boys? I think any mischief has been blasted right out of you.'

'We're sorry, Erin.'

It was the first whisper she'd had out of either of them.

She'd run a bath, washed them to within a whisker of their lives, rubbed them dry on Matt's mother's sumptuous white towels—and still managed to leave a streak or two of grey on the gorgeous linen—and then cradled them into bed. They shared the one bed, despite there being twin beds in the room.

In times of trouble these two stuck together and they were sticking together now.

And all the time they'd stayed silent.

Now, dressed in some very strange and ill-fitting pyjamas, they looked up at her from their shared pillow, and their eyes were still glazed with shock and fear and remorse.

'We only made the bomb to scare Pansy,' William said, trembling, and if he hadn't sounded so pathetic Erin might have been tempted to laugh. Oh, heck… Pansy Poodle?

'Why on earth would you want to scare Pansy?'

'So Mr and Mrs Cole would move away and stop being nasty to you.'

That was all she needed! She was overtired and overemotional and now she had to blink back tears. They were such terrors but there was always a motive. They had such good little hearts.

Somehow she schooled her features into sternness, and hugged them both.

'Well, we were very, very lucky that Mr McKay came to save us. You'll promise me you'll never, ever play with fireworks or matches again? Not even to scare Pansy?'

'We promise,' Henry told her and she looked down and knew that she had their word.

It wouldn't be a bomb next time. Something else for sure, but not a bomb.

She tucked them in, hugged them again for good measure and wondered where Tigger was now. They loved

Tigger, and when they realised he'd been burned... It didn't bear thinking of.

Then she looked up at the sound of footsteps in the hall. Matt was standing in the doorway. He was clean now, big and bronzed and capable, dressed in clean jeans and an open necked shirt and with only the burn on his forehead to show any damage had been done.

He was back to the farmer she knew.

Charlotte was one lucky lady, Erin thought suddenly. A class above the likes of her or not, Matthew McKay was not bad as husband material.

Not only was he extremely good looking, with his thatch of sun-bleached brown curls, his weathered skin and his strongly muscled frame, but his deep brown eyes were twinkling with kindness. In his hands he held two mugs, and he carried them carefully over to the bedside table for the boys.

'My Grandma always used to say a glass of warm milk is the best cure in a crisis,' he told the twins. 'So I brought you boys one each. There's another for Erin when she's had her shower.' And then he smiled at Erin—a smile that somehow had the capacity to knock her senses reeling. 'Off you go, and I'll meet you in the kitchen when you're clean.'

Darn, she must be more exhausted than she thought, Erin decided. She really was very close to tears, and his kindness was almost her undoing.

'I've also brought my very favourite story book from when I was seven,' he told her, motioning to a book tucked under his arm. 'It's all about fire engines. So I propose that you go and clean up while I read to the boys.'

'Your throat...'

'Hurts,' he finished for her. 'Well guessed. I'd imagine yours does, too. Luckily my book's mostly pictures so the

boys and I just have to look. So scoot.' He smiled down
at the two nervous little boys in their shared bed, and his
smile was encompassing and kind. 'Is that okay with you
guys?' he asked them. 'It seems a bit unfair that we're
clean and Erin's not.'

The boys considered in silence—and then slowly nodded in unison.

'Great.' Matt's smile widened and he sank down onto
the bed beside Erin. It was sort of crowded down there—
four on the bed—but it was familiar and very, very com-
forting after the fear of the last hours. 'I don't know about
you,' he told Erin softly, 'but I'm pooped and the sooner
we get this lot asleep the sooner we can get to bed ourselves.'

Absolutely.

He was perfectly right.

So why did his words bring a blush to her face as she
rose and headed gratefully to the bathroom?

And those tears were definitely still threatening.

By the time she'd showered, the twins were solidly, absolutely asleep. Wrapped in one of Louise's vast towels,
Erin checked them from all angles and decided it'd take
another bomb to wake them, and even then it wasn't a sure
thing.

She didn't blame them. She was exhausted herself, but
Matt was nowhere to be seen.

He'd meet her in the kitchen, he'd said, but she couldn't
go and find him wrapped only in a towel. Her own clothes
were disgusting, so she hauled on an enormous dressing
gown she found in the donations pile and made her way
through the house to find him.

The house was huge. Vast! It must have six or seven
bedrooms, she thought as she padded barefoot down the

passage, and when Matt emerged from a door in front of her she practically squeaked in fright.

'Hey, I'm no ghost.' Still those eyes twinkled as he put his hands on her shoulders to steady her. 'Uh, oh. You're done in.'

'You must be, too.' She looked up at him and saw that his eyes were still reddened slightly from the smoke and the burn on his forehead had blistered further. 'You look a darn sight worse than me.'

'I'd have to agree there.' The laughter lines deepened as he took in her total appearance. 'But only just. What you're doing in a bathrobe that looks like it was designed for Mother Hubbard...'

That brought a chuckle. The robe was enormous. She swam in it, and it trailed out behind her like a flannelette bridal train.

His voice softened as he realised why she was wearing it. 'Hell! I guess you'll have all lost your own clothes.'

She had. She'd barely had time to take it in yet, but it was something she'd have to face. Most of her belongings were back in the blackened, smouldering ruin. However...

'They were just things,' she said resolutely, trying not to think of her mother's seed pearl necklace that she'd loved so much. 'Things can be replaced.'

'You're one brave lady.'

'No.' She shook her head. 'I've never been so frightened in my life as I was this evening. I thought I'd lost them.'

'The boys.'

'Yes.' He was leading her into the kitchen as they spoke, and at last she relaxed. Unlike the rest of the house, this felt like a proper home. The kitchen had ancient polished floorboards, big comfy furniture, a huge wooden table and cushioned chairs, and a settee than made you want to bounce and sink out of sight.

A gleaming Aga was sending out its gentle warmth across the kitchen, and an ancient collie dog looked quizzically up at her as she entered. He thumped his tail gently against the floor and then went straight back to sleep.

This was home, she thought. This was a real home.

Damn, she had to blink back tears again. The waterworks were surely ready to pounce tonight. The fear had driven every ounce of strength from her.

Bed.

She should go to bed, but...

'Hot chocolate and a brandy,' Matt was saying. 'I know I told the kids warm milk, but you and I need something stronger. I've eaten toast. Do you want something to eat? No? Then just a drink and then bed.' He turned away to fetch mugs and glasses, and while he was faced away his voice changed.

'You love them, don't you?'

'Who?' She leaned against a chair to steady herself—her legs seemed to have lost all their strength—but she knew instinctively who he was talking about. His next words confirmed it.

'The twins.'

The hot chocolate made, he turned back to her and gestured for her to sit. There was nothing for it. In her ridiculous night wear she sat, sinking into his squishy chair like she was drowning. She took the chocolate and cradled it, drawing strength from the warmth of the mug.

She thought of the twins and her mouth twisted. 'I'm pretty fond of them.'

'You're a House Mother,' he said, thinking it through. 'I thought you're not supposed to get attached to your charges.'

'You mean I'm not supposed to care if they go up in flames?'

'I didn't mean that.' He was watching her face. 'The boys are different, though, aren't they? To you.'

She shrugged. 'I guess.'

'Why?'

That was harder to answer. She thought about it and gave him the easy answer. 'It's probably because they've been with me more than most. Kids don't tend to stay in orphanages any more. They get adopted or fostered out as soon as we can find someone who'll take them. Fifty years ago we used to have scores of orphans. Now we have kids like Tess and Michael who are in for short-term crisis care, or the baby Lori's taken for me. She's been with us while her mother made the decision to allow her to be adopted.'

'And the twins?'

'That's the problem. We can't find anyone for the twins.'

There. It was said—the stark reality that hurt just to think of it.

'Why not?' Matt said, watching her face.

'I don't know.'

'Liar.'

She shrugged, and then gave him a weary smile. 'No. I'm not a liar and I do find it hard to understand. They're adorable. But the twins push people away, you see.'

'I don't see.'

'You may well see it soon.' She sighed. 'Look, they were the product of a one-night stand. Their mother doesn't remember who their father is, and she has seven other kids to look after. To be honest, the twins reached their mother's IQ level when they were about three. I'd reckon whoever fathered them wasn't lacking in the intelligence quotient and they're smart as paint. Anyway, she can't cope with them, she rejected them absolutely and she threw them at us for adoption. Unfortunately they were old enough to understand what was happening.'

'And they're taking it out on the world?'

'Only on whoever is deemed to threaten them. And now they expect to be rejected. They won't let anyone close because they know it'll end.' Erin sighed. She was bone-weary and the comfort of the hot chocolate and the sympathy in this man's eyes was more than enough to push her over the edge. He'd poured her a brandy but she wasn't game enough to drink it. Her eyes wanted to close so badly...

'Sleep,' he said, and leaned over and took the mug from her hands before she dropped it. 'You'll find toothbrushes and everything you need in the bathroom.'

'I already have.' Her tired eyes smiled. 'Your mother must have been the best hostess in the district—and you haven't let her standards slip one bit.'

'I'm not allowed to.' He smiled back at her and his weary smile touched something in her insides which hadn't been touched in a very long time. If ever. 'Charlotte's trained the redoubtable Mrs Gregory for me, and she sees to it that everything's pristine.'

'Uh, oh.'

'Don't worry.' Before she knew what he intended, he reached forward and took both her hands in his. He pulled her to her feet and then stood for a moment, looking down into her troubled eyes. 'I'm sure you and me and the twins and Mrs Gregory will get along just famously.'

And Charlotte? Erin added under her breath but she didn't say it. Instead she looked up at Matt, a crease of worry still behind her eyes.

'Doc Emily said I should keep an eye on you tonight. You did lose consciousness.'

'I did,' he agreed gravely. 'But I don't want checking

every hour, thank you very much. If I promise not to die in the night, will you promise to go and put your head down on the pillow and let tomorrow's worries wait until tomorrow?'

Those dratted tears... Damn, they threatened to be her undoing.

She blinked and sniffed and then blinked again.

'Fine then. Um...you *have* put something on that burn?' She was under no illusions that Charlotte would kill her if it got infected.

'I have at that,' he told her. 'It's cleaned and it's nicely antiseptic. So we can both go to bed with a clear conscience. Goodnight, Erin.'

'Goodnight, Matt. And...thank you.'

And then, because she looked so rumpled and lost and forlorn he couldn't help himself. He leaned forward and let his lips brush her forehead.

'It was all my pleasure,' he said softly. 'Now stop thinking about twins and burns and belongings and worries. Think only about yourself for a change. Sleep!'

And she did.

There was simply no choice.

CHAPTER THREE

'WHERE are we?'

Erin planned to wake the minute they woke, but she must have been too exhausted for her normal House Mother instincts to work. She'd propped open both bathroom doors so the twins could see her as soon as they opened their eyes, and now they landed on her bed in a tangle of legs and arms and astonishment.

'Did the house really burn down? Did we really ride in a police car?'

That was easy.

'It did and you did and you're now at Mr McKay's farm,' she said, hugging them to her and hauling them in to lie under the covers. She was wearing an oversized T-shirt, and in their oddly assorted pyjamas they looked just as disreputable as she did. They were like something out of a charity bazaar, she thought and grinned to herself and hugged harder. She didn't mind. They were safe.

'The policeman won't arrest us?' It was Henry, ever the anxious one.

'Now why would he arrest you?'

'Because we made a bomb.'

'But you've promised faithfully never to make another one,' she said.

'Mmm.'

She fixed Henry with a look. 'You did promise.'

'Yeah.' He gave her a feeble smile. 'Okay. We did.'

'Then I think we might persuade him not to arrest you—this time.'

Apparently this was satisfactory. They snuggled down beside her and then snuggled some more.

But then William asked what was apparently super important in both their minds.

'Erin, where's Tigger?'

Oh dear. Erin thought back to the last she'd seen of the house. There seemed not one snowball's chance in a bushfire that anything could have been saved. There was nothing to do but tell them the truth.

'Guys, I'm afraid Tigger was burned.'

That silenced them completely. They lay, taking in the enormity of it, and then Henry sniffed.

One sniff was all he allowed himself, but Erin's heart wrenched. Tigger had been given to the boys by one of their first foster families—a sort of sop-to-conscience-at-taking-them-back-to-the-orphanage gift—and they'd been so young they'd mixed him up with leaving their mother and their bothers and sisters. Tigger had become their only constant, a toy never fought over, never discussed, but simply there.

Apart from each other he was all they had—and now they'd lost him.

Erin knew enough to acknowledge he was irreplaceable. She thought of the impossibility of saying they'd find another Tigger, and she simply didn't know what else to say.

She was saved by a knock. There was a light rap on the door and it opened to reveal Matt. Unlike Erin and the boys, Matt was fully dressed in his farmer's moleskins and khaki shirt. A sticking plaster lay across the burn on his forehead, but otherwise he looked completely unscathed. He was bronzed, strong, capable and ready for the day's work.

'Good morning,' he said gravely enough, but his deep brown eyes twinkled at the sight of the three in the bed.

'That's a single bed and you guys look squashed. Didn't you find the other two? Is something the matter?'

'We just came into Erin's bed now—to keep her company,' William said with dignity, casting a doubtful look at his twin. Henry was looking dangerously close to tears, and the twins' code of conduct decreed it didn't do to show emotion in front of strange adults.

They'd learned early to keep themselves to themselves.

But after one knowing look at Henry, Matt mercifully changed the subject, seeming not to notice the one errant tear sliding down Henry's cheek. He chose the one subject that might make them think of something other than loss.

'I've made pancakes and I thought you might like them in bed. How about it?'

'Pancakes?' William said, resolutely putting aside the vision of a burning Tigger. 'I...I guess...'

They were very upset about something, Matt realised, but he could only go on from here.

'I'll bring in a tray, shall I?'

'Yes, please.' Erin was so grateful she could have hugged him. How had he guessed that the last thing they needed was a formal breakfast? 'That'd be lovely.'

'Coming right up.' He left them to it, and Erin never knew what an effort it had been for him not to sit down and hug the lot of them.

It had cost to get them breakfast.

Matt had come in from the paddocks to find his weekly housekeeper, Mrs Gregory, hard at work. He had a cow in calf in the home paddock and, after a sleepless night, he'd decided he'd be happier checking on her than staring at the ceiling. His cow now safely delivered, he'd come in to find Mrs Gregory already sniffing lugubriously over the marks on the carpet.

'Charlotte rang me,' she said before he could say a word. 'I knew how it'd be, so I decided it was my Christian duty to get here early. Those dratted children. You saved them, didn't you? Why you had to offer to take them in…'

'I guess it was my Christian duty,' he told her and she didn't even smile.

'Hmmph. Those twins. And that mother of theirs. Oh, you don't need to tell me a thing about that woman. The whole of Bay Beach knew her before she disappeared with the last of her string of men. If ever there was a no-good, two-timing—'

'Hey, you can't place the sins of the mother onto the children,' Matt interceded. 'She threw the twins out.'

'Which is saying a lot about the children,' Mrs Gregory said soundly. 'That woman's a slut, and if even she couldn't put up with them…'

Hmm. 'Mrs Gregory, how would you like a holiday,' he said thoughtfully. This wasn't boding well for the future at all. 'Erin's here and, with two adults, she and I can surely do the housework.'

'She won't. She won't even notice if the house is a mess. I know her kind.'

'She will.' His lips tightened. Heck, his mother and Charlotte and their set had truly branded Erin. Just because of her father…

He finally wrung pancakes out of Mrs Gregory—by throwing in a few more Christian duties and an agreement to take an extended break for as long as they could manage without her—and now he carried the tray toward the bedroom with the air of one who'd achieved a major triumph. When he saw the grateful smile in Erin's eyes the feeling grew, so his chest felt a whole six inches broader.

There was still something wrong, though. Something

majorly wrong. The twins were polite—sort of—about the pancakes but they sat up in bed with the pancake tray on the table between them and they poked at Matt's offering as if the end of the world was nigh.

'You didn't yell at them because of the fire?' he asked Erin, frowning as she crossed to the window with her pancake plate. She'd done it as a deliberate ruse to talk to him without the twins hearing and it worked. He'd figured it out and followed her. Now they stood with their backs to the twins, as if the cattle grazing in the paddocks was taking all their attention.

She took umbrage at his suggestion. Yell at the twins? 'Of course I didn't,' she told him. 'They feel dreadful enough without me yelling at them. What do you think I am?'

'Far too kind,' he told her promptly, and she smiled but in an absent sort of way as she munched her pancake—which told him her thoughts were still on the twins.

'I'm not.' She glanced back at the twins. 'Sometimes I feel I'm not kind enough. They need so much...'

'Why the sad faces? Are they still scared?'

'No.' She shrugged, After all this man had done for them it seemed stupid to let him see how upset they were about one small Tigger, but there was something in his eyes that said he really wanted to know. He cared. 'It's just that they had a stuffed toy that they loved. They've now realised it's been burned.'

He stared.

Then...

'Wait right here,' he told them soundly, and without another word he strode from the room and left them gaping after him.

And then he was back, and in his hands—at arm's

length because it was so disgusting—he carried the blackest, filthiest soggiest *Tigger* they'd ever seen. But it was…

'Tigger!'

Erin barely got the word out before the boys were out of their beds, upending milk as they went and heading straight for Matt. They clung to what he held out to them— one to Tigger's snout, one to Tigger's tail, and all the grime in the world wouldn't have made one ounce of difference to the love that shone from their eyes.

Their Tigger…

Erin was looking at him as if he'd produced a miracle, and the feeling was just great. His expanding chest almost popped the buttons on his shirt. 'How on earth did you rescue Tigger?'

'I never meant to,' he told her and managed a shamefaced grin. 'They thrust it at me in the fire and, to be honest, I thought it was a dead cat. I just shoved it down my shirt and kept going.'

'A dead cat!' Her lips twitched. 'And do you always go around shoving dead cats down your shirt during house fires?'

'Before anything else. They're excellent for curing warts,' he told her. 'All you need is a graveyard and a full moon. Everyone tries to find them, but this time I got there first.'

He was ridiculous. She chuckled and suddenly things were just fine. The twins were inspecting their disgusting toy with relish. It appeared that the grime and general dishevelment made not the least difference to their affection.

How could it?

Matt grinned, trying to ignore the warm feeling Erin's pleasure was giving him. 'Doc Emily deserves some credit, too,' he admitted. 'She saw it when she was listening to my breathing and told me to hang on to it. Then I forgot it—until I took a shower, opened my shirt and it fell out. The damned thing nearly gave me a heart attack.'

'I imagine it might.' Erin's smile was a mile wide. 'We're so lucky you didn't toss it away.'

'I could have.' Matt's eyes were resting on the twins. They'd sat on their shared bed again, one end of Tigger on each of their knees. 'But by last night both Doc Emily and I had an inkling that whatever could be saved might be important.'

'You have no idea how important,' she said warmly. 'Oh, Matt...' Her eyes were glowing.

Whew! Her eyes were doing something to his insides which was truly spectacular. He needed to be grounded here.

He was.

The admiration session was interrupted before his chest buttons could finally pop from the strain. Just as Matt was starting to feel very peculiar indeed, another knock sounded through the room.

Visitors were coming thick and fast this morning, Erin thought, but what the heck. They had Tigger. With Tigger, they could save the world! They could cope with anything.

But it was Charlotte, and suddenly Erin wasn't so sure if anything included Charlotte.

She was amazingly early, Erin thought, and then she glanced down at her wrist-watch and stared in disbelief. It was after nine o'clock. Help!

And she looked like this!

'Charlotte,' Matt said warily, and the tone of his voice summed up all of their feelings.

Charlotte gave him her most sympathetic smile—heroine racing to save hero!—and then she moved straight to practicalities.

'Mrs Gregory told me you were feeding the children

their breakfast in the bedroom,' she said briskly. 'Why on earth don't you do it in the kitchen? At least you can wash the floor there.'

And then she looked again—and saw Tigger. She physically flinched.

'What…what on earth is *that*?'

'It's Tigger,' Erin said, and beamed her joy with the world. Even Charlotte couldn't burst her bubble this morning. 'He's a bit fire-stained. As we all are. Hi, Charlotte. Isn't it the most wonderful morning?'

Erin's greeting startled Charlotte out of her composure. 'I suppose it is.' She looked Erin up and down—aristocrat to a low life form somewhere under the level of porriwiggle. 'What on earth are you wearing?'

'At a guess, I'm modelling old Mr Harbiset's hand-me-down dressing gown,' Erin told her, refusing absolutely to be ruffled. 'He's the only local I can think of who's fat enough to own a dressing gown this size, and Mrs Harbiset's always giving things to charity.' She gave a fast twirl, ballerina-like, and the flannelette dressing gown swung out almost full circle around her bare legs. 'Isn't it great? You think the style will take off?'

Charlotte somehow managed a smile. Then she turned to face Matt, excluding Erin and the twins nicely from her ordered world.

'Matt, darling, I've talked to my parents,' she told him sweetly, in a tone that said she'd solved all his troubles. 'And they've been terrific. They say the orphanage can have the use of the stables until the Home is rebuilt.'

'The stables?' Matt blinked and Erin raised her eyebrows politely. Stables?

'I don't mean the stables proper, silly,' Charlotte said, giving him the benefit of her delicious, tinkling laugh. She threw the twins a look that said she wasn't so sure that stables wouldn't be the best place for them, but then went bravely on. 'No. There's living quarters directly above the horse boxes. We used them for the men when I housed all my horses there, but now I've moved out they're empty. They're still quite liveable.'

'That's very generous of your parents,' Matt said, thinking it through. 'But the living quarters were built for use by the stable lads, weren't they?'

'Yes.'

'Then they're pretty basic.'

'Yes, but it's almost summer.' Charlotte beamed. 'There's a little kitchenette and a dormitory and a bathroom. Everything they need.'

'One dormitory?'

'Yes.'

'So Erin would be sharing the dormitory with the children?'

'That's what she does, sweetheart.' Charlotte gave Erin her very nicest smile. Her beam widened, all her problems solved and she reached out to take Matt's hand. 'She won't mind, darling. Caring for children is her job. Isn't it, Erin?'

Hmm. Erin might have continued to twirl but she had also been listening. And thinking—fast.

'It is,' Erin said thankfully. 'And I'm very grateful. But I'm afraid I can't accept any offers before our director comes down here and sorts things out. Meanwhile, if Matt's offer still stands…'

'When's your director coming?'

'This morning, I imagine,' Erin said dryly. She glanced at her watch. Tom Burrows had been in Sydney this week, but she'd imagine news of the fire would have him down here by lunch time. 'I'll pass on your offer to him and he'll come out and see your parents—and the stables.'

'Hey, hang on a minute!' Matt wasn't having a bar of this. 'The kids are staying here.'

'You must see that's impossible.' Charlotte was still at her sweetest.

'Why?'

She lowered her voice, just enough to make the twins aware that they were being discussed without them hearing.

'Because they're juvenile delinquents, that's why. They burned down the last place they stayed in. Heaven knows what they'd do here.'

But that was enough for Erin. Her hackles had well and truly risen. Juvenile delinquents? *At seven years old?*

If she didn't get rid of this woman soon she'd lose her temper—which maybe wasn't such a good idea, she thought, as she'd really, really like to stay here for a while. This set-up was perfect for the twins. They had a farm where they could be relatively isolated from the rest of the community.

If Tom agreed—and he surely would—then she could stay here, too. The farm was beautiful, nestled right on the river mouth and overlooking the sea. It'd be like a beach holiday. There'd be no other children for her to look after—the Homes couldn't ask Matt to look after any more—and they'd have her sole attention.

Which was just fine by her. These were badly traumatised children, and most of the trauma had been inflicted well before last night.

'Matt, would you mind if you continued this conversation with Charlotte outside?' she managed. Juvenile delinquents indeed! 'I...I need to get dressed.'

'I noticed your donated clothes pile is still out in the hall,' Charlotte said pointedly. 'You'll have to go and forage. Unless you're planning on wearing what you had on last night.' She smiled.

'Charlotte!'

Whoops! She'd gone too far. Charlotte's self-preservation instincts surfaced then, as a look on Matt's face told her that he wasn't seeing things as she was. And this crazy woman wasn't any real competition. Matt was only being charitable, after all, and it behoved Charlotte to appear the same.

'I'll fetch you something, shall I?' she asked. She looked at Erin, assessing. 'You're a couple of sizes larger than me or I'd lend you something of mine.'

'I'm quite happy with our charity pile,' Erin said through gritted teeth. Anonymous charity, that was. Not Charlotte charity. 'I'll fetch something myself.' She pulled open the door and stopped short.

Last night, when they'd come here their toes had sunk into the lush white carpet. It had still been here and squish-able when she'd come to bed.

It still was now—but there was plastic over the top.

Lines of plastic. Erin recognised it. She'd seen it last at the home of a super-fussy aunt. Purchased by the yard, the stuff was transparent and it had tiny pointy teeth on the back to hold it to the carpet. People used it to keep homes immaculate against any who might sully their precious flooring, and it felt just horrid.

Urk! What was the point of having carpet if one had to look at it under plastic and walk on the coldness of the stuff?

She took a deep breath and counted to ten under her breath. She had to take this in her stride. Okay, it was insulting, but if Matt wanted to protect his home, then who could blame him?

But it wasn't Matt who'd laid the plastic. 'Where the

hell did that come from?' he demanded, staring. He stalked out into the passage and stared some more. The plastic tracked off in both directions, a path for anything unclean.

'I had heaps stored at home,' Charlotte said, not hearing the low growl of displeasure in his voice. 'I bought it when I went overseas last year and my grandparents borrowed my house. Grandpa is such a grub—he just refuses to take his boots off and Grandma doesn't insist. It was just the thing, I thought, and it worked beautifully but now Grandpa's gone and I don't need it. So I brought it over.'

She sounded immensely pleased with herself—but Matt had had enough.

'Well, you can just roll it all up and take it back where it came from,' he managed, embarrassed to his back teeth. Hell, of all the insensitive, unwelcoming acts. What would Erin think of this? Charlotte might be gorgeous and a great hostess and cook, but sometimes she was impossible. She really was just like his mother!

But...

'Um...no.' It was Erin.

'No?' They both turned to stare at her.

'Leave it. The kids and I will hardly notice.' The kids certainly wouldn't. A floor was a floor as far as the twins were concerned and Charlotte was right. This way Erin wouldn't sully Matt's precious carpet, and she wouldn't have to worry about the twins doing it either. Which was one less worry—and she had enough worries as it was.

But Matt was implacable. 'The plastic goes,' Matt told her. 'Now.'

'Matt, it's fine.'

'Erin, it's not!' His temper was rising now, and there were memories flooding back that were making everything worse. His mother standing at the kitchen door yelling at his father in the voice of a fishwife. *'Get those boots off right now or I'll walk out and never come back.'*

It was her ultimate threat made over and over again, it had scared the young version of Matt stupid, and only later had he wondered whether maybe he and his father would have been a whole lot happier without her.

Which might be why he was still a bachelor.

So no, the plastic went. And the image of marriage that he'd had last night faded a little as well. Maybe he was meant to be a bachelor. He'd bought the ring, but he hadn't done the asking.

But this was hardly the time for dredging up old memories and future plans. Now was the time to take the well-meaning but misguided Charlotte by the shoulders and steer her out of the room.

'We'll leave you in peace,' he told Erin. 'Charlotte, Erin's right. We need to continue this discussion outside.' He gave Erin and her crazy, wonderful dressing gown one last glance and then he propelled Charlotte outside.

'I'm going into town,' he told Erin over his shoulder as he left. Then he turned back to the lady he was propelling. 'Charlotte, I could use some help. Do you have time to come with me?'

Charlotte was surprised but instantly gratified. 'Of course I do, sweetheart. When do you want to go?'

'Now,' he told her. 'Erin, just make yourself and the twins at home. Mrs Gregory will be here until lunch time, so anything you need, just ask. Charlotte and I will probably eat in town so I'll see you mid-afternoon.'

Charlotte visibly sighed with relief. This was much better. A lunch date with Matt, with Erin nicely excluded. She turned and gave Erin her sweetest smile, because she could afford to be charitable to one who was so clearly a charity case—and then she allowed herself to be propelled from the room by the man she intended to marry.

There was no threat here, she decided.

There was no threat at all.

CHAPTER FOUR

Matt arrived home at about three and he couldn't find them. There were no kids in sight, and there was no Erin.

He walked from living rooms to bedrooms. No one. He went outside and checked the out-buildings. He checked that Erin's car was where it had been parked the night before and still he couldn't find them.

Finally he checked the house once more, and this time his old collie, Sadie, decided to join him. As they passed the laundry, Sadie whined and put up a paw. He pushed the door open—and there were the three of them, sitting on the floor with three noses pressed hard against the glass of the tumble dryer.

They were watching the tumble dryer?

'Isn't the television working?' he asked dryly, and they swivelled to face him.

They really were the most ill-assorted trio! The charity bin hadn't been good to them, he thought. Nothing fitted anywhere.

Yet Erin looked amazing!

He hauled his eyes from her with an almost Herculean effort. Concentrate on the twins! he told himself.

The twins were wearing jogging suit pants that were way too big, and T-shirts that were far too small. Their sea-green eyes were over big and over bright in their anxious faces and, as they looked up at him, he felt his heart give a thump of sympathy. They looked such waifs!

But Erin...

He failed. Try as he might, he couldn't turn his eyes from her. She didn't look much less waif-like herself.

She was wearing someone's cast-off crimplene dress—pale blue with pink spots, buttoned to the waist and belted with a cheap and nasty plastic belt. The dress looked as if it was meant for a woman of sixty. The bust size was about five sizes too big for her and it looked ridiculous. How she managed to still look beautiful was beyond him.

'If you so much as smile, you're dead meat,' she said, reading at least some of his thoughts, and he wiped the tentative smile from his face, hoped she hadn't read the rest and tried for a look of innocence.

'Now why would I smile?'

'Because this is—or was—Beverly Borridge's second-best Country Women's Association dress, and it's the only thing I can fit into. Her breasts must be…'

She faltered as his eyes fell immediately to the points in question. She blushed bright pink, she folded her arms defiantly across her chest and she turned back to the dryer.

'Huge,' she finished, but she was no longer looking at him.

He couldn't help it. He grinned—which was exactly the wrong thing to do, because she sensed it. She turned back and caught the grin full on and retaliated just like Erin had retaliated as a kid at school. No one teased Erin Douglas without copping it right back.

A sodden towel was lying by her side. How convenient. Her lips twitched into a smile, she lifted it and she threw with deadly accuracy. It whacked him with a soggy thwump; slap across his face.

She was some shot.

She was some lady!

But, soggy or not, he still didn't know what they were doing. Matt removed the towel from around his shoulders, laid it aside, wiped the grin from his face and crossed to the dryer. Once more, they all had their backs to him and they were staring at the dryer.

There was nothing for it but to see for himself. He crouched down beside them and stared at the glass.

'What's the program here?' he asked. 'Something good? *Days Of Our Lives*—or *General Hospital*?'

The twins simply ignored him. After that one brief glance they'd gone straight back to watching the glass window. Their anxiety was palpable and they were watching the glass as if their lives depended on it.

So Matt watched, too, and he saw a pair of eyes flash past the glass. And also a tail.

All was suddenly clear. 'That's Tigger,' he said in amazement.

'Of course it's Tigger.' Erin nodded and went right back to Tigger-watching. 'I rang the manufacturer. I hope you don't mind me using your phone but it was important to get his washing instructions right. They said he'd never dry naturally, even if we hung him out in the sun—he'd go mouldy inside. Their advice was to wash him in soap and water—and you can't imagine how much soap and water we had to use to get him clean, then squeeze him dry in a towel. We hung him outside in the sun long enough so the fur fabric was dry enough not to shrink, and then we put him in the dryer. But...'

'But?'

'But the boys are still a bit anxious,' she told him. 'We sat outside with him while he hung on the clothes line and now we thought we'd just stay here and watch.'

'I see.' The whole process was crazy. He repressed the grin, though. One look at the little boys' faces was enough to make that easy. Then he looked at the dial. It had twenty minutes to go. 'How long have you been here?' he asked.

Sitting watching tumble dryers going around ad infinitum was hardly his idea of a great afternoon's entertainment.

'An hour and a half. He should be almost done.' Erin had a twin on either side of her and she hugged them hard. She was acting like she had all the time in the world and this was the world's most pressing problem. 'And he's doing just fine.'

It might just as well be television's *General Hospital* they were watching, Matt thought. Drama had nothing on this. *Here we have the patient on the operating table and anxious relatives fearful of the worst...*

'He doesn't like it in there,' Henry whispered, and Tigger's eyes flashed past the glass again. Matt almost had to pinch himself back to reality. Good grief! This was a stuffed animal, yet the tremor in Henry's voice had him imagining agony within.

Twenty minutes to go...

'I brought back ice-creams,' Matt said helpfully, but no one moved.

'I'll fetch them, shall I?'

'That'd be great,' Erin told him, but all eyes were on the glass. They had no time for him at all.

If anyone told Matt he'd spend twenty minutes watching a stuffed animal go round and round in a tumble dryer—and almost enjoy it—he would have said they were crazy, but that was just what happened next.

He placed a chocolate ice-cream in the twins' hands, gave one to Erin and settled back with his. He should have brought popcorn, he thought. He hadn't realised they were into movie-watching.

They certainly were. There was hardly a word spoken. Every ounce of the boys' concentration was directed at

Tigger—as though by watching him they could get him through this ordeal.

They were amazing kids, Matt thought, and began to see what Erin was fighting for. Once you had the loyalty of these two, you'd have it for life. They licked their ice-creams, but they licked them absently and one flicker of doubt that things weren't well in the Tigger department and the ice-creams would have been abandoned. There was no doubt of that at all.

The ice-creams demolished, Tigger spun on and on, and then the timer clicked off. Tigger thumped three more times around the drum and Erin opened the door.

'He might be hot,' Erin warned but, hot or not, they'd waited long enough. The twins had him out of there and were checking him from snout to tail.

'He's perfect,' William breathed.

He wasn't, actually, Matt thought, looking at the battered toy that had seen years of loving service. Patches of Tigger's fur were completely worn off, his eyes were decidedly crooked, there was a piece missing from one ear and a bit of stuffing was coming out of his rump.

'Absolutely perfect,' Erin agreed, grinning from ear to ear. 'And I've never seen him so clean.' She poked the stuffing back into his rump. 'Wasn't it clever of Mr McKay to save him? I'll sew his bottom up tonight but meanwhile…'

'Meanwhile, now he's fixed, can we see the farm?' Henry said, bounding up and turning pleading eyes from one adult to another. With Tigger restored to glory, things were obviously okay in his world and he was ready to move on.

'Yes, please,' breathed William, and Matt looked into their combined eyes and could no sooner deny them than fly.

Plus Erin was watching.

'Haven't you been outside yet?' he asked.

'Apart from sitting under the clothes line, no. We had to fix Tigger first,' Erin told him, as if he was a little bit thick for not realising it. 'But now Tigger's better so maybe we can explore. If it's okay with you, Mr McKay?'

Okay?

Of course it was okay, and suddenly Matt was very, very pleased that they hadn't explored without him. He very much wanted to show off his farm to this woman.

And these boys, he told himself hastily. Not just Erin.

Of course not just Erin.

'What have you done with Charlotte?'

They were walking across the yard toward the machinery shed. The boys were whooping ahead, the traumas of the night before forgotten completely as Tigger circled victoriously above Henry's head.

'She's gone home to make dinner for me.'

'I see.' Erin didn't see. She was feeling acutely uncomfortable in her ghastly crimplene, but there was nothing else for her to wear. At least she had her own sandals, she thought gratefully. The twins hadn't even got those, and were now wearing wellingtons two sizes too big.

'I was supposed to be going there for dinner last night,' Matt said, and he also was feeling uncomfortable. After all he'd asked Charlotte to do in town, and the effort she'd put into doing it, he'd felt obliged to accept her dinner invitation.

There was also the issue of the little velvet box...

Whatever he decided about that damned box, he *was* putting Erin and the boys up only because they had no place else to go. That was the *only* reason. Therefore, as

Charlotte had carefully explained, he surely couldn't be expected to play host. And Erin wouldn't be lonely.

'Tom Burrows is coming out to see you,' he told Erin, and if his voice was a bit too gruff she appeared not to notice.

'Tom?' Tom was the director of the homes and Erin could only be grateful. She needed his advice 'You saw him in town?'

'I went to find him,' Matt said. 'He has heaps to do, you understand, but he said he'd bring pizza out from town at about six. He says he needs time to talk to you and that seemed the best way. He's caught up with insurance assessors until then but he wants to...' Then he caught his breath. 'Uh, oh.'

The machinery shed door was open. The twins had darted in and they were up on the tractor before Erin and Matt reached the door. Matt could only feel the keys in his pocket and think gratefully that nothing worked without those keys.

Unless...

They weren't old enough to have learned hot-wiring? he thought uneasily, and Erin looked up at his face and grinned. She really was a mind reader.

'No, they don't know how to hot-wire machinery. You know, they're not as bad as they're painted. It's just that they're two active, enquiring little boys, they haven't had the supervision they've needed in the past, and they need to be kept busy.'

'So my tractor is safe?'

'I didn't say that exactly,' she admitted—and grinned. 'Keep your keys locked up.'

'Yes, ma'am.' He smiled down at her, and something stirred within. She looked ridiculous, he thought, as the weird feeling kept right on stirring within his chest. Crazy

in her oversized crimplene and curls that he suspected
would tangle two minutes after brushing.

But she also looked sort of vulnerable. And underneath
the crazy crimplene and riot of fair curls, she looked very,
very lovely…

'You were saying about Tom Burrows?'

'What?' It was a big effort to make his mind work on
that one when it was thinking about crimplene. Tom
Burrows. Who was Tom Burrows? His mind was wandering all over the place—or maybe it was just wandering to
one place…

Tom… Oh, right. Orphanage Director. Tom Burrows,
the guy who was coming here tonight with pizza while he
was having dinner with Charlotte.

Why on earth had he ever agreed to have dinner with
Charlotte?

Business! Plans! Future! Get your head screwed back
on, McKay, he told himself sternly. He had things he had
to tell this lady, rather than stand here like a dummy and
try to remember why he'd agreed to have dinner with the
best cook in the district—and the lady he'd bought a velvet
box…

'I told Tom you're welcome to stay here long-term,' he
told her gruffly. 'Until the Home is rebuilt.'

She paused at that, and turned to face him. Good grief!
Had he any idea of what he was offering here?

'Matt, that's really nice of you but have you thought it
through? Rebuilding might take six months.'

'That's no problem. There's heaps of room, the house
is underused, you need a roof over your heads and I'm not
putting you out on the street.'

'The twins can always go into one of our Sydney
homes.' But she sounded doubtful at that.

'You don't want them to, though. Do you?'

There was only one answer to that. 'No,' she told him. She sighed and looked up at the twins on the tractor.

Which was unusual in itself, Matt thought. He was looking at her, and really seeing her, crimplene and all, but she was totally focused on her responsibilities.

This was a bit of a new thing, as far as Matt was concerned. Good looking and eligible—extremely eligible— Matt wasn't accustomed to young women looking straight through him.

But there was no doubt about it. She was only seeing the twins.

'They haven't had much security,' she was saying. 'Bay Beach is mostly *it*, really. It's the only place they know. A big city would scare them.'

'And you'd miss them?' Still he was focused on her.

She took a deep breath. 'I only have them between trials of new foster parents,' she told him. 'I can't... I shouldn't get too attached. Maybe Tom will have organised another couple to give them a try.'

Maybe he would. The thought should have pleased Matt—but then there was a tiny part of him saying that just maybe having this woman and these kids around for a while would be fun.

And suddenly the thought hit home that life wasn't much fun any more.

Sure he had a great existence, he told himself, surprised by the drab thought that had just entered his head. He had one of the best farms in the district. His stud cattle were internationally renowned, and he had more money than he knew what to do with.

And he had Charlotte.

But...

But what? He really couldn't say. He could only react to what was going on right now.

William was in the driver's seat of the tractor and Henry was standing beside him. Tigger was propped up on the windscreen. They'd pushed every button in sight without result, and now Henry was hauling the gear stick, just aching to make something go.

Their aching was irresistible, and so was the need to give them what he wanted himself. Fun.

'I need to check the cattle in the bottom paddock,' he called up to them. 'I'm taking the tractor. Do you want to come for the ride?'

Would they ever? They stared down at him, their eyes as round as saucers.

'Is it okay with you?' Matt asked Erin. Maybe he ought to have asked her first.

But her eyes were glowing and he knew straight away that he'd done the right thing.

'Sure, it's okay,' she said, smiling her approval. And then she added a rider. 'But only if I can come too.'

'You…'

'It's a very big tractor and we can squash,' she said.

'There's no need. I really will look after them.'

'I'm sure you will.'

'Well, then…'

'Well, then what?' She put her hands on her hips. 'What, Mr McKay? Why can't I come?'

'You mean you *want* to come?'

'Of course I want to come. It looks great!'

It looks great… He tried to think of his mother—or Charlotte, for that matter—ever wanting to ride on his tractor and the thought just wasn't there to conjure. They never would in a million years. 'I guess you can,' he said at last. 'I just didn't think you'd want to.'

She gave him a look of blank amazement. 'Why on earth would I want to be left behind? It looks really, really fun.' She swung herself up into the tractor cab and beamed down at him, a twin at each side. A conspiratorial trio, ripe for adventure, he thought, and he felt stunned.

There were four if you counted Tigger...

'Can I have a go at steering?' Erin asked. 'Please?'

They all had a go at steering.

Matt had to take the long way down to the bottom paddock because a couple of minutes' steering wasn't enough for any of them. The tractor was huge. Matt usually used it for hauling heavy harvesting equipment, not for ferrying passengers, but these passengers were entranced and he couldn't figure out who was the most excited to be in the driver's seat—the twins or Erin.

The twins went first, of course, with Matt standing behind them carefully controlling their attempts at driving. Then Erin took the seat, and his arms had to lean over her shoulders, just as they had with the twins. But it felt...different.

It was the crimplene, he told himself sternly, feeling just a trifle dazed. He'd never been so close to a woman wearing crimplene.

But the crimplene wasn't exactly sexy. So why did it feel that it was?

Concentrate on cattle...

The cattle in the bottom paddock were fine. The tractor circled them three times, just to make sure. They circled the cow with her new calf twice, and then, reluctantly, Erin turned the wheel to return to the house.

She was enjoying herself so much! The ride had been wonderful. It really was the most gorgeous day, and they'd been stuck inside with Tigger-washing for most of it. The twins' faces were glowing, and she didn't want to usher them back to the white carpets quite yet.

'Maybe you could drive the tractor back to the house and we could walk,' she told Matt, but he shook his head.

'Nope. Not unless you want to walk the long way round. The paddock between here and the house is due for first hay cutting next week and I don't want you walking in it. There's too many Joe Blakes.'

'Joe Blakes?' The twins were fascinated, as they'd been fascinated by everything Matt said. In their eyes, Matt had achieved almost cult status—not by saving them last night, but by saving Tigger. They thought, simply, that he was the greatest, and they hung onto his every word. Now they waited with bated breath to hear what he had to say about Joe Blakes, and he didn't let them down.

'Snakes,' he said deliciously and they shivered. 'We breed great big slimy ones hereabouts, and they'll be all through that paddock.'

Instinctively the boys moved closer to Erin and looked nervously down at the ground around the tractor. But their small boy need for ghoul meant that it was fine—as long as they didn't have to get off the tractor!

'It's safe enough to walk through when it's cut,' Matt told them. 'But not when it's two feet high.'

'No.' They breathed the word as one and Matt grinned. And suddenly he, too, was reluctant to end the day so soon. There was still an hour and a half before Tom was due, and he was expected to leave for Charlotte's.

He did have things to do. This was a working farm, but...

'Tell you what,' he said expansively. 'Let's take this baby down to the river and have a swim. Henry, it's your turn to steer. Erin—give up steering. It's Henry's turn!'

She was like a big kid, he thought, and grinned. She gave a comical grimace and pouted as she relinquished her seat to Henry. 'Aw, rats!' But... 'A swim?' she said, and looked a question at him.

'Now, I know we haven't brought our costumes and we're all wearing our very best clothes.' That brought a chuckle from all of them. 'But the river here is the safest swimming hole for miles. You want to do it?'

Once again he thought of his mother and Charlotte—and then didn't think of them at all as Erin's face lit up with laughter and delight.

'I can't think of anything we'd like more,' she said definitely. 'Thank you, Mr McKay. That would be very nice indeed.'

It was.

'You mean we really can swim in our clothes?' the twins asked, as the tractor slowed at the river bank. Here the paddock dropped to a sandy curve—a gorgeous, golden beach leading down to the water's edge. The river flowed gently here, having almost reached the sea. It'd be tidal this close to the coast, Erin thought. The water was turquoise and glittering, sandy-bottomed and clear as crystal.

And the need to swim was now irresistible to all of them.

'I really mean you can swim in your clothes,' Matt said. 'Though you might be more comfortable in your knickers.'

'Are you swimming in your knickers?' the boys demanded of Matt, and Matt remembered enough about being a small boy to know they intended to do exactly what he did.

Matt eyed the lady. She eyed him back and, hell, he could see what she was thinking. She knew exactly what he normally wore when he swam here, and the thought was enough to bring a blush to a grown man's cheeks.

Hell!

'Um… I think I'll leave my jeans on,' he told them, and that decided it as far as the boys were concerned.

'Then we'll leave our pants on, too.'

'Fine by me.'

Which left Erin.

Erin was looking doubtfully down at her crimplene. There'd been no bra to fit her in the donations pile. The bra she'd been wearing the night before was still hanging on the washing line, so she had no cover underneath her dress at all. Heaven knew what crimplene would do when it was wet.

But there was no way in the wide world she was not going to swim in this magic place.

'What are we waiting for?' she said, laughing and shrugging her shoulders. Okay, she was taking a risk with her modesty, but what the heck? 'Come on, twins. Last one in gets to wash up after pizza.'

To Matt's surprise, the twins could swim like little fish, and Erin was like a dolphin circling around them.

'It's my one life skill,' she told him, surfacing but only up to her neck. Very carefully up to her neck. Her fears about the crimplene were justified the moment she hit the water. 'You can't be brought up in Bay Beach and not swim, and I take a personal pride in teaching every one of my charges to survive in water.'

They could do more than survive. The twins were doing handstands under water, their toes just breaking the surface as they competed to see who could stay under longest. It was a game that looked like it could go on for hours.

Matt stayed until he saw that they were safe and then he swam away from them, stroking his usual two hundred yards up river and then down again. In a way it was a relief—to get away from the lady with the responsibilities.

And the transparent swimwear!

As for Erin, she would have liked to join him, he knew, guessing instinctively that she'd long to stretch out for a good, long swim, but she didn't. She stayed and supervised her boys, taking her duties very seriously. He watched from a distance, liking more and more of what he saw.

There was a boat, an old wooden rowboat, moored on a roughly made jetty a hundred yards from where they were swimming. It fascinated the twins, and Matt watched as Erin laid down the rules. She could see their fascination, and she knew trouble when she saw it.

'The boat is out of bounds when Matt or I aren't with you,' she told them as their gaze swung instinctively and longingly toward it.

'I'll take you out prawning in it one night,' Matt called. 'That's what it's for.'

'When?' The twins were nothing if not direct and Matt had to smile. He'd been like this at seven himself.

'When the moon's right. You can't prawn with a full moon.'

'So meanwhile it's out of bounds.' Erin fixed the two children with a look. 'Promise me you'll leave it be.'

'Why?' They glared back at her, and Matt's grin broadened. Yep, these two were trouble, but you had to admire their spirit. And Erin was their match.

'Because it's dangerous to be in without adult supervision. The tide could take you out to sea.'

'But we wouldn't—'

'You might. And while you're living with me you obey my rules,' she finished, and she glared at them right back. They tried meeting her look head on, but finally they conceded. How had he known that they would?

'Okay, we promise,' William whispered reluctantly.

One down, one to go. Erin's gaze shifted. 'Henry?'

'I promise, too.' And Matt knew that the promise would

be kept. Trouble, he thought. Yep, they were trouble but they weren't bad kids at heart. It was just a matter of guessing what the risks were before they took them. And Erin was some guesser.

She was some lady!

Finally he swam back to her as the twins whooped and dived away, the boat forgotten—or at least put on the back-burner. As he reached her, she'd just surfaced from a dive herself. They were nose to nose, a yard apart, and suddenly the whole set-up was intensely…

What?

He didn't know what. He had no experience to describe the way she made him feel. She looked amazing, he thought, completely free of make-up, her blonde curls hanging in wet tendrils over her face and to her shoulders, and her eyes bright with sunshine and with happiness.

And this was a lady who'd lost everything only the night before?

Maybe her belongings had been in another place, he thought. He asked her, and her face momentarily clouded, the pleasure of swimming dissipating.

'Nope. The Home has been my home for years. I guess everything I had in the world was burned.' But then her face was deliberately cleared, blocking pain. 'But they were just things. I told you before, they can be replaced. We have the kids and we have Tigger. Who can ask for anything more than that?'

She wouldn't mourn if her white carpet was stained!

The thought crept in subtly at the edges and held. His house was full of beautiful things. How would he feel if they were destroyed?

Probably gut-wrenchingly dreadful, he decided, thinking of the paintings his mother had so carefully collected over her lifetime. To not care about things was an entirely new concept—as was the way he was looking at Erin now.

'Hey.' She was laughing, her lovely blue eyes twinkling at him over the water. 'You're looking at me like I just landed from Mars. I'm not that bad.'

She surely wasn't. Different, yes. A world apart from the world he lived in.

That, too. But not bad.

The boys had dived through the water to shore, and were up on the bank. Instinctively Erin turned toward them. She'd learned early never to take her eyes from them. Not for a moment.

True to form, they'd headed straight to the only threat as far as the eyes could see. There were two long pieces of wood on the shore, driftwood brought in by the tide. The sticks were worn by the sea to smooth, white poles.

'Hey, these'd make great swords,' Henry yelled, and lifted one up. William was almost as fast, and Erin dived away from Matt and was at the river's edge almost before the poles had touched.

'No,' she said sternly, but they tuned out as if they hadn't heard her. The poles clashed in salute and clashed again.

And then the fight was on in earnest. Robin Hood and Sheriff of Nottingham—without the finesse.

And without the Hollywood blunted swords. These sticks were big enough to hurt!

'*I said no!*' Erin was out of the water now, stalking toward them. She couldn't get close—the sticks were flailing wildly enough for her to be injured if she got in the way. 'William. Henry. You put those sticks down this minute or you will walk home. The long way or through the Joe Blake paddock. Take your pick.'

There was one more clash, but they'd heard her. The sticks slowed and their eyes grew thoughtful.

'You know I mean it,' Erin said, as if she didn't particularly care what they decided. 'You choose.'

They turned and stared at her, and Matt, who'd swum to the shore, watched the battle of wills with some surprise. This was a side of the twins he hadn't seen. They were being crossed, and they didn't like it.

He could have intervened, but he didn't. This was Erin's territory after all, he thought. She was the child expert, and she was facing them down with a sternness that told him she had every intention of following through with her threat.

'We want to fight,' Henry said, his voice mulishly stubborn.

'And one of you will win and one of you will be hurt. Those sticks are heavy enough to hurt badly,' Erin said. 'You heard me, Henry. Put them down.'

Henry turned to William. Their eyes locked and Matt knew they were asking a question of themselves.

And finally Erin won.

But not happily. As if of one accord, the boys glowered, then turned and threw the sticks as hard as they could across the beach toward the paddock beyond.

It was just unfortunate that Sadie chose that moment to appear from behind the tractor.

The old dog hadn't been with them during their tour—there'd simply been no room for her in the tractor cab—but she must have watched the tractor's progress from the house. When it stopped she'd plodded on down to the river to find them. Just at the wrong time.

William's stick caught her right across the foreleg. She gave one stunned yelp and collapsed. She tried to rise, yelped again and lay still.

No!

Matt launched himself up the beach like he'd been shot. His dog! His Sadie....

With one incredulous look at the twins, Erin followed him, her heart sinking to her toes. Dear heaven, just when everything was going beautifully...

It was always like this with the twins, she thought, her heart sick with dread. It was why no foster family would have them. Disaster followed them like sunshine followed rain.

'Is she hurt?' Erin couldn't see. Matt was crouched over his dog, his whole body tense, and all Erin could see was one black and white tail. It lay ominously still. She took those last few steps around him, and then sagged in relief as she saw the collie lift her head and look pathetically up at her owner.

It *had* been her foreleg, then. For one awful moment Erin thought maybe she'd been mistaken in what she'd seen, and the stick had caught her head.

Her leg was bad enough, though. It was bleeding sluggishly at the point of impact, and Matt's face was grim as death.

They'd be out of here tonight, Erin thought bleakly, as she looked down at the lovely old dog. And they deserved it. Oh, no!

'Matt, I'm so sorry.'

'So am I, but it's not you who should be apologising.' Matt's voice matched the grimness of his face. One hand was cradling the old dog's head, the other was carefully examining the injured leg. 'Maybe it's not so bad. I can't feel a break, and she's holding it up.'

She was, too. When Matt released the leg—just half an inch from the ground so it couldn't be further hurt if it fell—Sadie kept it up, as much as to say, *'Look at this, it hurts.'*

'She really is a bit of a hypochondriac,' Matt told Erin in an undervoice, so the twins couldn't hear. 'But it was a fair whack. She'll have to be checked.'

'I'll pay the vet's bill.' Heaven knew her wages weren't sufficient to cover all she'd have to buy in the next few weeks but this…

It was her fault, she thought bleakly. She should have seen the sticks. She should have moved faster.

She'd let herself be distracted by Matt…

'Erin, don't! I told you before, it's not you who should be apologising.' Matt cradled his dog and looked up at her. She looked so distressed that he couldn't bear it. Damn, she'd been through enough because of these kids.

She was so lovely. Standing there in her crazy crimplene that had turned totally translucent with the water, she looked…

Actually she looked naked.

Maybe he'd better concentrate on his dog—and on the twins, he told himself firmly. As Erin was so distressed, then it was time for him to take a hand in the twin-control stakes.

What these kids needed to learn was consequences.

But what?

The twins were standing side by side, ashen-faced and flinching. He looked up at them, and he knew instinctively that these kids had been beaten in the past. Beaten beyond reason. They weren't in an orphanage for nothing. Nobody loved this pair, and they knew it.

So now their faces were stoic, expecting pain. They were expecting the world to come crashing down around their ears, as it had so obviously done in the past.

What had Erin said of them?

They expect to be rejected.

They expected it now. They were waiting for a good thrashing and to be sent away, and a glance at Erin's face said she thought the same. Oh, not the thrashing—because she was here—but she was surely expecting him to toss them out.

'Come here,' he told them and then, when they didn't move, he lowered his voice a notch. 'Henry. William. I said come here. *Now!*'

With an uncertain look at each other they came. Slowly, their shoulders touching, they came, waiting for what was to come, but waiting together.

Erin's whole body tensed.

She was like a mother hen, Matt thought. If he laid a finger on these boys, no matter how justified he was, he'd have her to contend with, and he just knew that taking her on would be some task.

He was doing no such thing, but the boys had to face up to what they'd done.

'You've hurt Sadie,' he said, and waited for what most kids would say. *William did it*—or *We didn't mean to*, or *It wasn't our fault.*

They said none of those. Instead their faces fell to Sadie and the knowledge that had hit home when he'd watched them with Tigger in the dryer was reinforced yet again. These kids weren't bad. They cared. Their loyalty, once won, was won forever.

So no, he wouldn't thrash them, and he wouldn't throw them out.

'We...we're sorry,' Henry whispered and one glistening tear slid down his cheek. Only one. These kids had schooled themselves not to show emotion and it didn't show now.

'Being sorry won't help Sadie,' Matt growled, immeasurably moved despite his anger. 'You need to do something that will.'

'Like…' It was Henry again. William was trembling, and the urge to lift the child and give him a hug was almost overwhelming. Erin, though, was managing to hold her hug instincts in check. She was leaving this to him. 'Like what?' Henry whispered.

And Matt made a snap decision.

'We need to take Sadie to the vet to make sure the leg's not broken. I'll call first, but before that we need to get her back to the house. That means we all have to squeeze on the tractor because I'm not leaving Erin behind. You two climb up behind the driver's seat, sit down and make your knees as flat as you can. Then I'll hand her up to you. You'll carry her on your knees. You'll be uncomfortable but I can't help that. Erin, can you ride on the step?'

'Sure.'

Of course. Anything.

'Right. Let's move.'

CHAPTER FIVE

IT DIDN'T stop there.

Back at the house, Matt carried his dog inside to her basket, he telephoned the vet and then he turned to the boys. 'Okay, you have two minutes to get changed because you're coming with me.'

'But...' It was Erin and he turned to face her. His face was still implacable, but then she saw the tiniest glint of laughter behind his eyes and her own widened with astonishment.

'I'm pretty sure the leg's just bruised,' he told her as the boys disappeared toward their bedroom and dry clothes. 'But I've pre-warned Ted, our local vet. He'll play it up—as I suspect Sadie's playing it for all she's worth. She was hit by a car when she was a pup. I pandered to her dreadfully while she recuperated, and now every time she'd like a little snack—say when I'm eating a nice juicy steak—she'll look pathetic and limp.'

'Oh, Sadie...' Erin stooped down and hugged the big dog lying pathetically in her basket, her leg just slightly raised as if to say, *What a thing to suggest!—I'm fatally wounded here.* 'You wouldn't do that, would you?'

'She would.' Matt knelt, too. Which was sort of nice, he decided. Erin was still gorgeously transparent—literally—and kneeling beside her was quite an experience. 'That's not to say the whack by the stick didn't hurt, though. I bet it did. And now...' He patted his old dog's head. 'She likes the vet, we'll buy her some rump steak on the way home and the boys just might have a lesson in consequences.'

Erin took a deep breath. 'Thank you for not yelling at them,' she said softly, and he smiled at her.

Mistake.

She smiled back, and something strange happened. Something indefinable.

But real. Incredibly real.

'It's… It's my pleasure,' he told her in a voice that was suddenly none too steady. 'Now, if you'll excuse me, I'll go put some dry clothes on as well.'

That'd be good, Erin thought inconsequentially. He'd been swimming bare-chested, he was still bare-chested and crouched beside her he was suddenly far too large and far too…far too male!

And far too something she couldn't define in the least.

'Do you want me to come, too?' she asked. She should. They were her charges.

'No,' he told her, breaking the moment finally by rising and backing a step or two. 'This business is between me and the boys. You stay here and wait for Tom. There's enough on your plate without worrying about my dog.'

He was right, only…

'I should stay with the twins.'

'Delegate responsibility,' he told her, and just for a fleeting moment he touched her damp curls. That was a mistake, as it happened, because the 'something' that was between them intensified a hundredfold.

He caught his breath, and tried for a dignified exit. 'Just for an hour or so,' he told her. 'Just for a while, I want you to think of yourself and let me worry about the twins.'

He left her, but he didn't leave her thinking about the twins—or herself for that matter.

All she could think of was Matt.

* * *

'There was no harm at all in letting them go with him.'

It was Tom. The head of the Home Service had arrived at Matt's farm before Matt, Sadie and the twins returned from the vet, and Erin was feeling dreadful.

When she'd finally got her muddled thoughts back into order she'd gone straight back to concentrating on the twins, and now she was imagining the worst. What sort of chaos could they cause in a veterinary surgery? However, when she told Tom what was happening, his eyes grew thoughtful and he nodded his approval.

'Don't worry. Matt's a sound man, Erin,' he told her. 'I spent some time with him this afternoon, and by the end of it I decided he's the sort of person who, if he applied as a foster parent, I'd be approving in a flash.'

'There's not much chance of that.' Erin gave her boss a half hearted smile. 'You take one look at this house and you can see that. And when you meet the lady he intends to marry...'

'Was that the woman he was with this afternoon?' Tom's craggy eyebrows raised in surprise. 'Charlotte? I didn't know he was engaged.'

'I don't think he is yet,' Erin told him. 'But I gather marriage to Matt has been Charlotte's intention for years. She's knocked back perfectly good offers while Matt went out with other women. Faithfulness personified, is our Charlotte, and I can't see him letting her down now. In fact...'

She took a deep breath and wondered why there was a strange constricting feeling around her heart. 'I have a feeling there's an engagement ring in the truck right now. I saw something that definitely looked like a ring box. Maybe he was planning on popping the question last night.'

'I can't see it happening.' Tom shook his head. 'I took

to Matt right away, but I didn't take to her. She's a cold piece of work.' Then he smiled, relegating Charlotte to his list of the least of his worries. 'Nevertheless, she's useful for some things.' He motioned to the back of his car. 'She's great at shopping. She did all this.'

'All what?' Erin followed his gaze.

'Clothes shopping. None of the rest of us could do it. Lori's flat out taking care of the baby, all the other house parents have their hands full with problem kids and Wendy's taken in Michael and Tess. We knew you'd be desperate for a change of clothes, and you can't go shopping in welfare handouts. Matt remembered you were Wendy's bridesmaid, so he rang her to find your size, and we had the boys' on file. We bullied an emergency contingency cheque from the insurers, then Matt sent Charlotte shopping—and there you go.'

Erin stared. 'There I go?'

'More clothes than you can poke a stick at,' he told her. He lifted the pizzas from the passenger seat. 'Clothes courtesy of your Matt's organisation and his Charlotte's happiness to shop, and dinner courtesy of me. I hope this place runs to a microwave so we can reheat these when the twins return.'

'It runs to everything,' she said, staring at the parcels and itching to undo them. Matt had organised this? Was this why he'd had to take Charlotte into town? The thought warmed her to her toes, and made it difficult to concentrate on anything else.

Somehow she had to manage it. What were they talking about? Oh, yeah. Matt's house. 'Honestly, Tom, it's a display home,' she said at last. 'I don't see how we can stay here.'

'I don't see how you can do anything else,' he told her. 'It's an answer to a prayer. There's nowhere else I can put you. The only alternative is me laying you off for six months, leaving you unemployed and me sending the boys to Sydney.'

That was some choice! It sure took her mind off parcels. But even so...

'You're prepared to keep paying me as a House Mother if I stay on here?' Erin was incredulous.

'I am. I had an emergency briefing with the board before leaving Sydney this morning,' he told her. 'The problem's the twins and I told them that. They're getting too old to place. No one wants to take on two seven-year-olds with a history of trouble, and I won't separate them.'

'No.' The very idea was dreadful.

'Everyone wants babies,' Tom said sadly. 'I could place a hundred Marigolds. Littlies are easy but, once they're over six, people believe that the damage has already been done.'

'The twins are still...salvageable.' Erin said softly. 'They're still capable of attachment.'

'That's why I put your case so strongly to the board,' Tom told her. 'If we take them to Sydney they'll have to go into one of the bigger homes—even if it's only for a short while—and I hate the idea. It could do so much damage. We may have these kids on our hands for the long term, Erin. House Mothers are supposed to be short-term parents while we find foster homes or adoptive parents but it's not happening here.'

He shook his head, but he was watching her face and seeing acceptance of what he was asking. Even more commitment to the twins! 'It's asking a lot, and separation at the end will be more difficult, but the alternative's worse,' he told her gently. 'If you can care for them here for a while longer I'd appreciate it. I'll do my damnedest to find them some other couple as soon as I can, but it's looking bleak.'

'I don't have a choice then, do I?' Erin asked, and Tom shook his head again.

'No. Matt's offer is far too good to knock back. He's said he'll take you for the full six months.' He fixed her then with his all seeing look. Tom had been around, and he knew his staff. As he watched the trouble washing over her face, a sudden thought occurred to him.

'It's not putting you into an awkward position, is it?' he demanded. Then he brightened. 'I guess it can't be if the man's engaged to be married. There'll be no hassles.'

'No.' But she sounded doubtful.

He picked up on her doubt straight away, and he pounced. 'You don't trust him?'

'I trust him, all right,' Erin said, as she turned away with the pizza boxes. And then she added a rider that was meant for her ears only. 'I'm just not sure I can trust myself.'

'Her leg's just badly bruised. We didn't break it.'

They burst in like miniature time bombs, exploding into the kitchen with their news. Momentarily they paused as they saw Tom, but they'd been dealing with Tom all their lives and apart from lowering their voices a notch, it didn't stop them telling Erin what was important.

'The vet says it's just grazed and bruised, but he's wrapped it up in a great big white bandage and he says she's not to walk on it for a week.'

'Which is just what is going to happen.' Following the twins was Matt, carrying Sadie in his arms. He lay the big dog down in her basket, she looked pathetically up at him—and then she wagged her tail.

The wag destroyed the pathetic image completely and Erin had to grin.

'Not mortally injured, huh?'

'Not.' The boys had spotted the pizza which demanded their immediate and undivided attention—which left Matt free to speak to Erin and Tom. 'I'm glad to see you again,' he told Tom.

'It's my pleasure to be here.' Tom beamed at what was happening around him. A man, a woman, two kids and a dog. This was a great family situation. Perfect. If he'd tried to engineer a better placement for the twins, he couldn't have done it.

A sudden idea flashed into his head, his eyes grew thoughtful and his smile widened as Erin shooed the boys out to wash their hands before eating. Hmm.

Double hmm.

'I brought enough pizza for the lot of us,' he said expansively. He was suddenly feeling expansive. He was a man who liked a good happy ending if he could possibly arrange it. 'There are four different types. Help yourself.'

Then he watched Matt's face with interest—and he liked what he saw.

What he saw was confusion.

The pizzas smelled great, Matt had decided, but that alone was really, really strange. Matt was a bachelor and pizza was his staple food—except he'd become fed up to the back teeth with pizza. Normally he'd run a mile to avoid it, and something gastronomically wonderful was waiting for him at Charlotte's.

But suddenly all he wanted to do was haul up a chair, sit down beside Erin and eat pizza.

'Um…no.' He gave a half hearted grin. 'I have a date.'

'With Charlotte,' Erin told Tom, and Tom nodded politely. But his eyes were still thoughtful. His idea, once planted, refused to be dissipated by a small obstacle like a fiancée.

His idea was wonderful!

'Well, off you go, boy,' he told him. 'I daresay Erin won't wait up for you.'

'She certainly won't.' Erin's eyes creased into laughter. 'I'm pooped already. Too much excitement last night and then a swim on top of it... I wonder how you can face a night out.'

'But he's going to see the woman he loves,' Tom said, watching Matt's face and getting answers to unspoken questions that were most satisfactory. 'I expect he won't find that tiring in the least.'

The woman he planned to marry was waiting for him. She'd been ready for hours, and the cooking smells hit him before he opened the door of the truck.

Wow! They were great smells. And then Charlotte was running lightly down the front steps of her house, greeting him with a hug as he pushed open the door, and he had to acknowledge that she looked just beautiful.

'Matt. Darling. I thought you'd never come. No more house fires tonight?'

'No more fires tonight.' He put her away from him and smiled down at her. She really was incredibly lovely—and those smells...

But it wasn't quail.

'I thought you were reheating last night's dinner,' he said, suddenly uneasy. 'That's why I agreed to come—so it wouldn't be wasted.'

'Well, yes.' She blushed and fluttered her eyelashes at him. 'But...' Her eyes slid sideways. 'I sort of thought... Well, I saw the box when I was in the truck this afternoon, you see, and I thought lobster thermidor was the very least I could produce—and Dom Pérignon champagne to go with it.'

The box.

Hell, the box!

It was still sitting where he'd left it last night. Two thousand bucks' worth of diamond and it had completely slipped his mind. He'd had it sitting in the truck all day, and he hadn't even locked the truck! Or thought that whoever sat in the passenger side would see it.

And now...

Charlotte was looking at him with eyes that glowed, then looking past him to where the damned velvet box was still sitting in the map compartment. She was expecting him to ask her to marry him.

Well, why not? he demanded of himself, and wondered why he felt so reluctant to move further. This was what he'd planned to do all along, he told himself. He'd thought about it long and hard. It was the sensible decision.

But...the twins.

'Charlotte, I've offered to take the twins for six months,' he told her hastily.

'That's fine.' Apparently it wasn't an impediment.

It wasn't. Charlotte had heard Matt make his offer to Tom this afternoon and her mind had been working in overdrive since then. There was no way she wanted *that woman* living with Matt—but maybe she could cope with the twins. Just for a few months. If she must. All they needed was a little discipline!

'Tom didn't like our idea of the stables,' she said, in a voice that hinted at her opinion of orphanage directors who weren't grateful for any charity they could get. 'But I've been thinking about it. If Erin stays with you, there's a

Home Mother completely taken up with only two children. So what if we get married quite soon and look after them ourselves?'

For Charlotte this was a definite possibility. Unknown to her beloved, she'd had her wedding gown and her wedding plans ready for years. This would not be a rush.

'We could go away for a lovely honeymoon,' she told him, taking his hands in hers and smiling her most beautiful smile. I'm sure my manager here would take over your farm while we're away, and we'd be combining the properties anyway. Then we can come back and Erin could leave.'

He was stunned. 'You have it all figured out.'

'Mmm.' She beamed, and then looked into the truck again. The box was irresistible. 'It's so sensible.' She leaned in, lifted the box from where it lay, opened it and stared down at the solitary diamond. And gasped. 'Oh, Matt! It's just beautiful.'

But he was still uneasy. 'Charlotte, I don't know—'

'Look, let's not worry about the twins and Erin tonight,' she said, sliding the ring onto her finger with a triumphant flourish and tucking her arm in his with proprietorial ease. 'In truth, I don't know when I can organise the wedding, but I'll try to do it as soon as possible. For now, let's just concentrate on being engaged—and tackling our lobster and champagne. It's cost me a fortune and I refuse to let it spoil. For now we're celebrating our engagement. The rest can all be sorted out over the next few days.'

Hell!

How had he managed that? he thought as he drove home three hours later.

He was engaged to be married!

Well, he'd made the decision when he'd bought the ring.
He might have known. Charlotte probably had spies in the
jewellers. This town was too small for secrets, and even if
he hadn't left the damned ring in the truck she would have
known he'd bought it.

It was impossible to back out now.

And why would he want to?

He thought that through, forcing his confused mind to
be sensible.

This was a sensible, well thought-out decision, he told
himself firmly. Charlotte was a lovely woman and she'd
been faithful to him for years. She'd make a loving wife
and a wonderful homemaker.

She'd never appear naked in wet crimplene!

And he'd never want her to, he told himself but he knew
deep down that he was a liar. Or maybe he wasn't.

He wouldn't want Charlotte in wet crimplene—but Erin
was a different matter.

Hell!

He'd expected them all to be in bed. Erin wasn't. She was
sitting at the kitchen table, surrounded by opened parcels.
She was sorting clothes into piles, and as he walked in,
her eyes lifted to his and glowed with pleasure.

'Matt, these are excellent. Charlotte's been so good.
They're great, sensible clothes, the sort that we can really
work in around the farm. They're just what we need.'

He walked forward and fingered the clothes. Yep, they
were sensible. Jeans, T-shirts, windcheaters, sneakers...
Great for the boys.

Sensible for Erin.

But he sort of liked the crimplene.

Yeah, and he knew why. He grinned at himself and

thrust the memory of Erin in wet crimplene onto the back-burner. There'd be no more of that now. Charlotte had outdone herself. These were quality clothes, carefully chosen. Erin would look practical in these clothes; like a sensible, hard-working Home Mother. A woman who knew her place in the world. They wouldn't turn transparent when wet. They were built to cover everything!

Charlotte wouldn't be seen dead in these clothes.

That was an uncharitable thought, he decided hastily, pushing it away with a definite shrug. Charlotte wore quality linen blouses, and tailored skirts or slacks. He knew instinctively that Erin wouldn't like Charlotte's style of clothes, and these were much more...well, sensible. So she'd done the right thing. To criticise Charlotte's choice of clothes was to be unfair to the woman he'd just promised to marry.

Or...she was the lady he'd just seen put his ring on her finger, he thought suddenly. He'd never actually said the words, 'Will you marry me?'

He'd never actually promised anything.

It didn't matter, he told himself harshly. She was wearing his ring, and she'd wear it now for ever. Tomorrow she'd tell the world, and he should, too.

Starting now.

'Charlotte and I are engaged,' he told Erin.

Her eyes flew to his, there was the merest fraction of hesitation—and then she rose. Her pile of denim fell back onto the table. Erin's face creased into a smile of delight for him—she really did seem delighted!—and she walked forward, took both his hands in hers and kissed him lightly on the forehead.

'Matt, that's wonderful. I'm very, very happy for you. The whole town's been expecting it for ever.' Then she stood back a little, her eyes twinkling with understanding. 'It was supposed to happen last night though, wasn't it?'

This lady had the knack of knowing things he'd rather she didn't, but there was no point in denying what was obvious. It just disconcerted him. 'Yes.' He thought for a moment of telling her the rest of Charlotte's plans and then thought better of it. Weddings took ages to organise.

Please let it be six months....

Erin's thoughts were still on Charlotte, unaware of the threat the marriage posed to her boys. A Charlotte mother!

'Poor Charlotte,' she was saying. 'No wonder she looked so downcast yesterday. Matt, I'm so sorry we messed with your plans.'

He wasn't, and he wouldn't let Erin be sorry either. 'Hey, it got me lobster instead of quail,' he told her, and she chuckled.

Erin had the most delicious chuckle...

'And to think you missed out on pizza. Poor old you. Lobster and a new fiancée. Tch. And our pizza was Bay Beach's best!'

He grinned at her. Erin's laughter was infectious. 'Yep. It's a real shame.'

'Mmm.' Still she was smiling, and he suddenly could think of nothing else to say. All he could think of was how blindingly attractive her smile was.

Funny he'd never seen it before.

Maybe it was because he was engaged, he thought. Erin was now forbidden fruit. He was engaged to be married.

He was *happily* engaged to be married! Forbidden fruit indeed.

So he should leave. He should go to bed. Instead he stood, stupidly fingering the pile of new clothes.

'Charlotte's bought you everything you need?'

'Yes.'

'She should have brought you something pretty,' he said inconsequentially. 'You can't just wear jeans and wind-cheaters.'

'There's not a lot of call for me to wear anything else,' she told him bluntly. 'These are just fine.'

'But you go to dances and things.'

'Only when I'm off duty. I don't expect I'll be off duty for a while.'

'I can look after the twins sometimes,' he told her. 'If you want to go out.' He took a deep breath. 'Like tomorrow... Go to town tomorrow. There's still plenty left from Tom's insurance cheque. Go and buy yourself something nice.'

'I hardly need pretty things tomorrow.'

'You never know.' He stared down at the jeans with distaste, and noticed a pile of flannelette pyjamas. He looked more closely and discovered they were all the same. Charlotte had bought three sets of red flannelette pyjamas, two small pairs and one larger set. His mouth tightened in distaste as he lifted them for inspection.

'And these,' he said shortly. 'They're wrong. I don't know what Charlotte was thinking of buying matching sleepwear. They'll make you and the boys look like something out of an institution.'

Erin agreed, but she was forced to defend Charlotte. She had to be grateful. 'Matt, they're new and clean and the boys won't notice. They'll be fine.'

'They're not fine and I'll notice,' he growled, and her gorgeous chuckle rang out again.

'Oh, no, you won't. These are pyjamas, Mr McKay. Worn in bed. You need never see them.'

'I don't want to. They're dreadful.'

'They're sensible.'

'They'll be hot as be damned. It's almost summer. You're not wearing them.'

'Tonight I'll wear them.' Her eyes were defiant—but still twinkling. 'It's them or nothing—and I'm definitely not wearing nothing.'

Erin in nothing…

Where had that thought come from? Erin not in her crimplene. Erin in less…

Hell! He had to get out of here. He was a sensibly engaged man.

Just as well, or anything could have happened.

'We'll talk about it in the morning,' he told her. But he grabbed the package. There was no way he was letting her wear those pyjamas. 'Meanwhile, wear a T-shirt or something. These are going back to the shop.'

'Yes, sir.' Her tone was half mocking and he grimaced. Did she know what he'd been thinking—and what he was feeling right now? Somehow he knew that she did.

He glowered and glowered some more. 'Good. I'm glad you agree.'

'It doesn't mean I'm not grateful for Charlotte's thoughtfulness.' She wasn't, but she wouldn't admit it for worlds.

She turned to gather her clothing together, and he stood watching her for a couple of moments. Erin was wearing the dress she'd been wearing the night before when the home burned down—one of her Charlotte-decreed home-made jobs. It was pale blue with lemon swirls, with a couple of fire stains she hadn't been able to remove by scrubbing. Stained or not, it made her look…

It made her look as if the jeans and windcheaters Charlotte had chosen were totally unsuitable.

Suddenly he had a thought. This was one thing that was suitable, at least.

'Erin?'

'Yes?' She paused from her clothes gathering and looked up in enquiry.

She was expecting him to go to bed and leave her, he thought. She was expecting nothing from him at all.

He felt his midriff clench in sudden pain. Hell, he wanted to do something for her so badly, and all he had was this. He shoved his hand into his back pocket and found what he'd been searching for.

'Tom showed me the layout of your house and which was your bedroom,' he told her, his suddenly gruff voice failing to hide his inexplicable emotion.

'Yes?'

'There were a few things we were able to salvage.'

Her face stilled. 'It wasn't all completely burned?'

'The roof burned and the ceiling caved in,' he told her, seeing her sudden look of hope and wanting to dispel it before it started. 'The weight of the ceiling, and the soot and smoke and water effectively destroyed most of your stuff. But the base of your bedroom didn't actually catch fire. The roof caved in while it was still smouldering, but it was doused fast. So the lads from the fire brigade and I made a really good search and we found these.'

And he lifted up what he was holding—a string of seed pearls.

As pearls went they were what he'd been brought up to believe were inadequate. Both his mother and Charlotte would have scorned these as trumpery, he knew. But to Erin...

To Erin they weren't trumpery. She stared at the string dangling from his fingers, then took a tentative step forward as if she couldn't believe what she was seeing.

'My mother's necklace.' She whispered the words. It was as if she wasn't able to believe what she was seeing, and any minute they'd be snatched back from her.

'It's the only trinket we found that was recognisable,' he told her. 'Did you have much jewellery?'

'That's all I had.' She lifted it from his fingers and stared down at it, still disbelieving. 'Oh, Matt...'

'I'm sorry we couldn't retrieve more stuff,' he said awkwardly, but she lifted her face to his and her eyes were bright with unshed tears.

Then, before he knew what she was about—before he could take one step to defend himself—she threw her arms around his neck, raised herself on her tiptoes and kissed him soundly on the lips.

It was a kiss of thanks—nothing more. It was a kiss of gratitude.

So how it had the capacity to knock him sideways—to have him catch her waist in his hands and pull her in to him and kiss her back—to feel like his world was shifting on its axis and shifting forever—who could say?

Matt couldn't.

He could only feel, but feel he did. He felt the way her body felt delicious under his hands. The way her mouth yielded to his and the touch of her hair against his, the moulding of her breasts to his chest—the fragrance of her....

He didn't understand this in the least. He could only feel and feel some more, and when she finally pulled away he could only regret her parting, and regret it with every inch of his being.

'Oh, Matt, thank you,' she whispered, and the tears in her eyes were real now, threatening to slide down her cheeks. She blinked them back, fast and furious, and then made a grab for her pile of clothes. Carefully sorted heaps were ignored. They were crumpled into one vast mound of clothes, gathered against her breast almost as a defence.

'Goodnight, Matt.'

And then she fled, taking her clothes and her necklace twin-wards, before her tears finally were allowed to run free. She left Matt staring after her, wondering what the hell he'd just done.

He'd just restored a necklace to its owner.

And now something else needed restoring but it was nothing tangible. In fact, he didn't have a clue what it was.

But it was a long time before he slept that night. And when he slept, he didn't dream of the lady he was about to marry.

He dreamed of seed pearl necklaces, and he dreamed of Erin.

CHAPTER SIX

DESPITE the emotions of the day, Erin slept soundly. In fact, she slept more soundly than she remembered sleeping for years.

It was because Matt was here, she thought as she drifted toward unconsciousness. As House Mother she always slept on the brink of waking. There was always a child in need. And before that...

Her mother had died when Erin was just fourteen. Erin had been the oldest of the kids. Her father had crumpled with her mother's death so she'd reared her siblings with love and also, she had to admit, with pleasure. When the last child left home she moved on to being an orphanage House Mother, but her choice of career meant that from the time she was fourteen there'd always been a child dependent on her.

There was no one else to share her load.

But here, at the other end of the house, slept Matt. She wasn't totally in charge. The feeling was novel, and she shouldn't indulge it, but in truth it was also wonderful.

She indulged it. The twins slept soundly and Erin totally relaxed. She slept on dreamlessly, and she couldn't guess that at the other end of the house Matt stirred and tossed and fretted because he couldn't get her out of his head.

Erin woke at dawn when Matt crept silently into the room next door.

She might have been sleeping soundly, but she was still a House Mother. Some things were instinctive, and protection was one of them. The moment the twins' bedroom door opened, her eyes were wide and she was pushing herself up in bed wondering what was wrong.

She'd propped the bathroom doors open between the two rooms so she could see, and she could see clearly straight through. Matt was in his working clothes and he was tip-toeing towards the twins.

'What's wrong?' It came out as a whispered croak of surprise.

He cast her a look of annoyance—annoyance with himself for waking her. 'Hell, Erin, I'm sorry. You go back to sleep. I'm after the twins.'

She found her right voice. 'What on earth for?'

'The twins hurt my dog,' he explained. 'So I told them last night that they need to accept responsibility for what they'd done. Sadie needs to rest for a week, and therefore the twins need to take over Sadie's workload.' He reached the bed the boys were still sharing and touched two small shoulders. 'Okay, guys. Wake up. It's six a.m. You know what we need to do.'

And, amazingly, they did. They opened their eyes, they smiled shyly up at Matt as if this had been expected, and to Erin's astonishment, they moved straight into dress mode.

'What on earth are you doing?'

'Tell her, boys.' Matt smiled at her—and then he carefully diverted his attention elsewhere.

Hell! What was happening here?

Following orders, Erin was wearing one of the welfare shirts as sleepwear. It was buttoned to the neck and it was a man's shirt to boot, but the sight of Erin fresh from sleep, tousled and rumpled, with her curls flying free and her gorgeous blue eyes wide with enquiry somehow had the power to make something inside him kick.

Hard.

Luckily a twin spoke, giving him time to gather his wits.

'We're rounding up the cows,' Henry told Erin solemnly, hauling on the ill-fitting trousers he'd worn the day before.

'You have new clothes to wear now,' Erin told him, and then took on board what Henry had said. 'Rounding up cows?'

'The boys don't need new clothes to do what they need to do,' Matt told her, still carefully concentrating on the twins. 'In fact, new clothes would be completely wasted. We're cutting Cecil out from where he's been serving the cows. He's due at the Lassendale Cattle Show tomorrow.'

'The Lassendale Show…'

'You're still half asleep,' Matt told her kindly. 'William, that windcheater's inside out. Surely you know the Lassendale show, Erin? And you a farmer's daughter and all.'

Right. Of course she did. The whole farming world knew the show he was talking about, but she'd never been there. Well, why would she? Lassendale was a show-case of the cream of the country's pedigree cattle, and a prize from the Lassendale judges meant the making or breaking of a stud farmer. Of course Matt would be showing.

'You're putting Cecil in the show?'

'I surely am.'

And then Erin started feeling strange, too. Matt was adjusting William's windcheater and the sight of him dressing the little boy—a job she should be doing herself—did strange things to her insides. Things she didn't understand in the least. She hauled her bedclothes up to her neck in an instinctive act of defence, but for the life of her she couldn't think what she was defending.

'And the boys?' she managed.

'I can't cut a bull out of that herd without a good dog,' he told her, his eyes twinkling. He'd overcome his unease in the face of her discomfort—or maybe it was because she'd hauled the sheet up so far. 'Or, failing a dog, then two obedient twins. Which I have here, don't I, boys?'

'Yes.' William said the word solemnly and Henry nodded his agreement.

'Now there's no need for you to get up,' Matt told her. 'I'll give the boys some milk and a piece of toast each and we'll have a proper breakfast when we're finished. You go back to sleep.'

Back to sleep? Such a thing was unheard of. Go back to sleep when the twins were awake...

'No!'

'You're not wanted,' Matt told her, making his voice severe. 'Is she, boys? Cutting out bulls is man's work.'

'But Matt,' She was bewildered by the plan. 'A bull—'

'Cecil is a pussy cat,' he told her, seeing what her major worry was. 'Don't fret yourself. You know I wouldn't let the boys near anything I considered dangerous. With these two to help me, we'll have him back to the yard in no time. Then we'll scrub him down, make him beautiful and then we can introduce him to you personally.'

'But—'

'Stop arguing and go back to sleep.'

'Matt—'

'Sleep!'

Sleep? Ha!

Go back to sleep, he'd said, but it was just plain impossible. Erin lay in bed and listened to the sounds of the boys in the kitchen. She heard Matt talking, and she heard the boys giggling in response.

Giggling?

They sounded just like they did when they were plotting trouble, Erin thought, but the difference here was that Matt was plotting trouble for them. Excellent trouble. Cutting a bull from the herd was just the sort of adventure they craved, and to do it with such a wondrous person as Matt...

He was wondrous, Erin thought sleepily. He knew instinctively how to act with the boys.

Take responsibility for your actions...

She'd tried and tried to drum that into them, and here was Matt doing exactly that. Yesterday they'd hurt Sadie, so today they were doing Sadie's job.

She desperately wanted to join them, but she knew that to do so would spoil it for them. This was men's work, Matt had decreed, and for Erin to interfere... To have their House Mother hovering over them, fussing and bossing while they did it, would spoil it in a way she instinctively understood. So somehow she forced herself to lie still.

Then the bedroom door opened again and it was William, carefully balancing a cup of tea.

'Matt said you'd like this.'

Behind him was Henry, carrying a plate of toast with marmalade. Erin blinked and blinked again. Breakfast in bed! Good grief!

And Matt was in the doorway behind them, watching his charges with pride as they wobbled their responsibilities to her bedside table—without a single spill.

'Well done, boys,' he told them. He looked at Erin and he winked. 'Okay, lady. Wrap yourself around your breakfast, then put your head on the pillow and sleep—while we men go off and organise the world. Okay, men. Let's go round us up some beef cattle.'

She couldn't do it.

She physically couldn't lie in bed and do nothing. It

nearly killed her. She drank her tea and ate her toast, then
lay and stared at the ceiling for all of half an hour. Then
Sadie sidled in and put her nose on the bedcover, and Erin
fondled the old dog's ears and smiled in sympathy. She
knew exactly what the dog was thinking.

'We've been made redundant, girl,' she said softly and
Sadie waved her silky tail in agreement. 'How does that
make you feel?'

Sadie flopped down on the mat beside the bed, put her
head on her forelegs and sighed.

'It makes you feel funny, too?'

Another sigh.

'I suppose I could just go see what they're doing,' she
told the dog. 'From a distance.'

Sadie looked up at her with hope, and Erin shook her
head.

'Not you, girl. You have a sore leg to look after.' Then,
at the look on Sadie's face, she burst into laughter. 'Oh,
you fraud. You pulled a con and now you're feeling like
you'd like to change your mind.' She leaned down and
lightly touched Sadie's bandaged leg. 'I'm sorry, girl, but
you're going to have to put up with it. I have a feeling
your leg might be more important than you know.'

There was another sigh at that, and Erin was starting to
feel like the dog understood every word she said. Which
was good, because Erin surely needed someone to talk to.

'I know how you feel,' she told her. 'But for more reasons than one, you need to keep your nose out of it.'

But Erin wasn't keeping her nose out.

If she stayed in that bed any longer she'd bust something.

If there was one thing being brought up on a farm with
seven siblings had taught her, it was how to hide. Years

of hide and seek had made her a master of the art. Erin washed and dressed with speed, and then made her way down the paddocks, moving from the concealment of one clump of river gums to another with the ease of a master.

The mustering team—Matt and his dog-cum-twins—were easy enough to find. The boys were whooping and yipping loud enough to wake the fishermen back in Bay Beach. Their targeted herd of cows was moving uneasily away from this unknown quantity, and by the time she reached the edge of the paddock where they were, Erin had a clear idea of what Matt was doing.

He was using the boys just like he'd use a working dog. Maybe they didn't have as much finesse as Sadie possessed, but his team strategy was effective all the same.

It was simple, really. Matt would send the twins into the herd, whooping at the top of their lungs and effectively splitting it down the centre. Half the herd would move one way, and Matt would concentrate on keeping the half containing Cecil the bull packed tight into the fenced corner. Ignoring the rest, they then had a smaller herd to work with.

Once the herd was where Matt wanted, the twins moved in again to split a smaller herd. With each foray of yipping and yelling, they made the controlled group smaller.

And finally there was just Cecil, a confused-looking beast but a magnificent specimen of Hereford Bull all the same. He stood in his corner, a twin at each side and Matt before him. While Erin watched from her safe distance, Matt slipped a rope through the ring in the bull's nose. The huge animal looked up at Matt in a resigned sort of way, and then he started plodding steadily toward the house before Matt so much as tugged on the rope.

He'd done this a thousand times before, his body lan-

guage said, and while he might have tried his darndest to
escape, now that he was cornered, like Matt had said, he
was a real pussy cat.

So much so that Erin wasn't surprised when Matt
slipped the rope into Henry's hand so he could lead him,
and then scooped William up to ride on the bull's broad
back. The twins were so light the bull would hardly notice
his burden.

He didn't. Cecil plodded on without changing stride.

'You ride halfway, and then swap with Henry,' Matt
told them, and from where she stood in the cluster of gums
by the paddock's boundary, Erin could see the twins' col-
lective shoulders expand a notch or six.

They'd be so proud of what they were doing!

All their attention was on the bull. Henry was leading
the bull with the solemnity of an undertaker leading a fu-
neral procession, and William was clinging on as if he
expected Cecil to buck.

And, as she watched, Matt fell behind, then turned his
head toward the trees where Erin was hiding, and he
waved. And grinned.

Caught!

For a split second Erin hesitated, then she grinned and
waved back. Drat the man, he had eyes in the back of his
head.

She wasn't wanted, though. She could see that. She left
them to it, and went quietly back to the house.

She was a House Mother without charges, and it felt
very peculiar indeed!

By the time they finished doing what they were doing, she
was fed up with being a House Mother without charges.
She desperately wanted to be part of it.

The urge to go out to the sheds was almost overwhelming. Instead somehow she made herself organise the boys' clothing, make the beds, prepare another breakfast, talk to Sadie, talk to herself...

'I'm going nuts,' she told the dog. 'I don't think I'd be very good at living alone.'

She'd been alone for three hours and it felt weird.

'What are they doing out there?'

She didn't know, and Sadie couldn't help her. So they sat in the kitchen and waited, and it was hard to know which of them was more frustrated.

Finally they reappeared.

They were filthy! The twins were mud splattered, soaking wet and they were beaming from ear to ear. They stood at the back door and fought for the rights to tell her everything. All at once.

'We've cleaned him and soaped him all over and now he shines and shines.'

'He's beautiful.'

'I rode on his back.'

'William squirted Matt with the hose but he didn't mean to, and Matt didn't mind...'

Then Matt appeared behind them, and he was just as filthy as the twins were—and his grin said he was just as happy with his morning's work. He smiled at Erin and then looked doubtfully down at himself.

'We're a bit dirty to come in,' he told her.

She nodded, trying not to laugh. They were all so pleased with themselves, but that mud...

'I think you should stay outside,' she told them.

'Aw, Erin...' Both twins howled a protest and then saw she was laughing. Their small faces relaxed and they took a tentative step over the threshold.

'Stop this minute!' She stopped them in their tracks, in

a voice that Charlotte or Matt's dead mother would be proud of. 'Go not one inch further.' Matt blinked. He hadn't thought it of her.

And he was right. She wasn't worried about her kitchen floor. She was concerned about something else.

'Do you have a camera?' she asked, and when he nodded she made him tell her where to find it.

'Because you're not getting rid of one spot of that gorgeous mud until I've documented this moment,' she told them. 'I want a photograph of you guys standing next to a beautiful Cecil so I can remember this moment for the rest of my life.'

It wasn't just a memory for Erin.

She took the photograph from three different angles, with Matt standing proudly, one hand on each twins' shoulder, and all beside Matt's magnificent, gleaming bull, and she knew this photograph would be precious for many reasons.

The boys had so few memories. So few possessions.

If she took copies of this and framed it, it'd become as valued as Tigger the Tiger, she thought, and she finished taking the shot and raised her eyes to Matt in gratitude.

'Thank you,' she said and her words held a whole wealth of meaning.

He got it in one.

'My pleasure,' he told her and if his voice wasn't quite steady it wasn't for the want of trying.

Then they trooped through the kitchen, showered, the boys inspected and accepted and donned their new clothes and they breakfasted properly. They sat at Matt's big kitchen table and wrapped themselves around bacon and eggs, and toast and cereal, while Erin watched with amazement at what they were demolishing. The boys were normally picky eaters. Now they ate and talked and ate and talked like there was no tomorrow.

And all the time Matt watched, like a benevolent genie who'd wrought this change with a wave of a magic wand.

They were great kids! he was thinking. The best!

'Do you like your new clothes?' Erin asked, and they nodded over slices of watermelon. Matt had done a vast grocery shop the day before, and he'd done them proud. He'd had to do a few things since he'd granted Mrs Gregory her holiday, but he was finding that he didn't mind in the least. The house was the cosier for it.

It was also messier. Matt looked ruefully down at the tracks he and the twins had made across the kitchen floor which Mrs Gregory wouldn't have tolerated to stay while she cooked breakfast. But it was definitely cosier.

Nice.

'But we don't like your clothes,' Henry was telling Erin, and Matt agreed entirely.

'What's wrong with mine?' Erin looked down at her beautifully fitting jeans and long-sleeved shirt. 'They're great.'

'You wear dresses,' Henry said stubbornly and William tilted his chin in agreement.

And Matt found himself with the kids. Yep, Erin wore dresses. She looked great in dresses, even the crimplene.

'Go into town and buy yourself something decent,' he growled. 'Now. Today. I can look after the twins.'

'My dresses are home-made,' she told him.

'So? My mother's sewing machine is still here. Buy yourself what you need and I'll twin-sit while you sew.'

'We'll help,' the twins announced, and Erin grinned at the thought that conjured up.

'Oh, great. I can see a twin sewed into each side of the zipper—with Sadie's nose at the bottom.'

They chuckled at that, but Matt wasn't to be side-tracked. 'Seriously, Erin…'

'Mmm?' It was time for her to tilt *her* chin.

He tilted his right back. He could be obstinate, too. 'The clothes Charlotte bought were just to tide you over until you got a wardrobe you liked.' He glanced at his watch. 'The draper's open on Saturday afternoon. You could go in now.'

'But the twins—'

'The twins and I have more work to do,' he told her. 'And I'm more than capable of looking after them by myself.' Then he paused at the sound of a car pulling up outside. He knew that sound. 'And maybe I don't have to,' he continued. 'Here's the help I need.'

It was Charlotte.

Of course it was Charlotte, and Erin schooled her face into an expression of pleasure. After all, Charlotte had shopped for her, and she was Matt's affianced wife. The fact that Erin had never been able to stand the woman should be irrelevant. So as Charlotte walked into the kitchen—without knocking—she found Matt and Erin smiling a welcome, and the twins looking up from their bacon with expressions of distrust.

The distrust was nothing new or personal. The twins distrusted the world.

'You're still eating breakfast!' Charlotte, as beautifully presented as ever in her smart slacks and blouse and beautifully arranged chignon, stopped on the threshold and stared at them all in amazement. Her eyes fluttered to the delicate silver watch on her wrist. 'Matt, darling, it's ten o'clock!'

And then she saw the mud on the floor, and her breath drew in horror. 'What on earth has been going on?'

'They've been cleaning Cecil,' Erin told her, rising and crossing to the woman at the door. She kept her smile straight, took Charlotte's hands in hers and kissed her lightly on the cheek before Charlotte could pull away. 'I hear congratulations are in order. You're engaged to be married! That's lovely news, Charlotte. And you're not to be disgusted with us. This is our second breakfast—and the mud is Cecil mud.'

'Cecil...' Charlotte thought this through and her face cleared. 'Oh, the bull. Of course. You've been cleaning your wonderful bull for tomorrow's show. But, Matt, you know you should have stripped at the door—or made the children do it at least.'

She regarded the twins as one might regard two interesting but slightly disgusting creatures from the sea, and it took an almost Herculean effort for Erin to keep her smile pinned on.

'It'll only take minutes to mop, but the troops were hungry,' she told her.

'Well, I guess it was in a good cause,' Charlotte said reluctantly. 'As long as you do intend mopping, Erin. I don't see that Matt has the time. We're leaving at the crack of dawn tomorrow.'

'You're *leaving*?' It was Henry, his eyes swivelling toward Matt. His face was horrified.

'I'm taking Cecil to the show,' Matt told him. 'It's a two-day affair so I'll only be away for one night.' His brow creased. 'I didn't think you were coming, Charlotte?'

'I've managed to find a place at the hotel,' she told him. 'The Royal's very expensive, but it still has places.' She gave her tinkling laugh, the laugh that made Erin shudder. 'I thought...now that we're engaged we should do things together.'

Urk. The boys winced, and inwardly Erin winced along with them. Charlotte's sweetness was almost repelling.

And it seemed Matt found it almost as distasteful. He dredged up a smile and rose, carrying his plate across to the sink.

'Well, that's great.' Then he turned back to Erin, and his face was under control again. 'Erin, now that Charlotte's here, I want you to hop it. Go into town and do your shopping.'

'But what for?' Charlotte looked from Erin to Matt and back to Erin. 'I did all the shopping you could possibly want yesterday.'

'And it was wonderful,' Erin told her, but Matt shook his head.

'Charlotte, if everything you owned in the world was destroyed by fire, could you imagine another woman supplying you with everything you need on one shopping trip? Without even discussing it with you first? You don't think that Erin might just want to buy a couple of things herself?'

'I guess…' Charlotte faltered at Matt's logic, but she obviously didn't. In her view, Erin was a charity case, and charity cases deserved what they got.

But Matt was no longer listening. 'Go, Erin.'

'I'll just clean up—and the boys can come with me.'

'No.' Matt's voice was implacable. He took her shoulders, steered her to the door and forcibly propelled her out. 'Charlotte and the boys and I will clear up, and then we'll take hay around the cattle. We'll be so busy we'll hardly miss you. I don't expect you back here before four o'clock. So go.'

She cast one worried look at the twins, but Matt wasn't taking no for an answer.

'If you're sure…'

'I'm sure. And so's Charlotte. Aren't you, sweetheart?'

Charlotte was stumped. There was nothing for a well brought-up young woman to say to that but yes, and she rose to the occasion with fortitude.

'Of course.' Charlotte gave them all her very sweetest smile. 'You go and do your shopping, Erin. I'll look after your responsibilities.'

Drat the woman!

Erin's hands clenched on the steering wheel all the way into town, and by the time she got there she was still having trouble calming down. What Matt saw in that cold-blooded barracuda... Couldn't he see what she really was? She was so nice to Matt, but so darned nasty to those she didn't consider important.

It was nothing to do with her, she told herself, as she drove into Bay Beach. Matt's love life was Matt's business, and that was that.

She was here to shop.

And then she saw Shanni emerge from the greengrocer. Her face brightened. Shanni was a really good friend. Like Erin, she was a local girl from a farm where money wasn't in oversupply and so, like Erin, she'd been given the cold shoulder by Charlotte from a very early age. What Erin needed now was a coffee, a chat with her friend and a very long whinge.

'Where are the kids?' she called, and Shanni beamed as she dumped her shopping in her car and headed across the car-park to her friend.

'They're at Mum's. Oh, great. I was just going to head out to see you. You want a coffee and a chat?'

'Do I ever,' Erin told her. 'If you don't mind a bit of bitchiness thrown into the gossip.'

'That's my very favourite kind of gossip,' Shanni said, and tucked Erin's arm into hers. 'What gives?'

Back at the farm it was Matt's temper that was giving. He'd loaded the trailer with hay, the twins had helped cheerfully enough but when they headed out to the paddocks Charlotte decided she was coming, too.

Then, as William heaved his first bale off the trailer— no mean feat for one so small—she told him how to do it right.

'The cattle trample it if you put it down in full bales,' she told William sharply. 'Wait until Matt cuts the twine and then throw it off a quarter at a time.'

William's small face fell, he dropped behind the trailer and Henry, after looking at his twin, decided to do likewise.

They stumped along unwillingly, waiting to go home. Charlotte scolded. Matt tried to make things right but the more that was said the more the twins turned stubborn and mute.

'You'll be glad to get away tomorrow,' Charlotte told him. 'Kids are okay in small doses—in very small doses.'

'They're good kids.'

'If they were good kids they'd have been adopted long before this.'

'Hush!' Charlotte's voice was carrying. Matt cast a glance behind him. He didn't think the twins had heard, but… 'Be a bit careful of what you're saying.'

'I'm only telling the truth,' Charlotte said stubbornly. 'For heaven's sake, they actually burned down a whole house. They should be a bit grateful for what you're doing instead of grumping along like two spoiled brats.'

Yeah. Right. But they didn't look like spoiled brats, Matt thought as he tried to cheer them up. They just looked like kids who knew they were hopeless and expected to be told that at every available opportunity.

'Come and help me brush Cecil,' he told them as they finally fed out the last of the hay. 'He'll be dry by now, and he needs to be brushed like he's never been brushed before if he's to win.'

'Oh, Matt, really...' Charlotte again, unable to resist putting in her oar. 'As if they know the right way to brush a bull. I'll help.'

'Boys...'

'I want to watch TV,' Henry said, and William chewed his bottom lip and said nothing.

'I'd really appreciate it if you could help me.'

Silence.

Erin arrived back at the farm feeling very much better. There was nothing like venting a little spleen with a friend, she thought cheerfully as she turned into the gate. That, a couple of bolts of material, a really gorgeous ready-made dress, new shoes and a bottle of her favourite perfume supplied by Shanni had made her feel she was ready to face the world again.

Or ready to face Charlotte.

They were in the kitchen. Erin pushed wide the door and knew they'd been talking about her. The conversation stopped dead as she entered, and Matt bit his lip.

It wasn't anything good, Erin thought, but then, when had Charlotte ever said anything nice about her? Or anyone who had less money and influence than Charlotte?

'Hi,' she said brightly, determined to be cheerful. 'I had to come home. Bay Beach ran out of things I could buy.'

'Did the insurance money run to all this?' Charlotte asked incredulously, looking at Erin's parcels. She sniffed.

'That's the same perfume as Sally wears. It costs a mint. And you've never bought a dress from Della's!'

'I do get paid,' Erin said gently. 'I'm not exactly a welfare case, Charlotte.' She dumped her parcels and somehow kept right on smiling. Then, because she knew it'd cut right to the bone, she couldn't resist. 'I even had money left over for lacy knickers. Because a girl just never knows...' And that was enough of that! 'Where are the boys?'

'They're watching television,' Charlotte snapped, watching Matt's face and not being reassured at all. He'd definitely heard what Erin said, and there was definitely a level of interest there. 'They've been distinctly unhelpful.'

'I expect they're tired,' Matt threw in, trying to appease—and trying not to think of Erin in lacy knickers—but Erin was no longer listening. She left them to each other.

If Matt was stupid enough to believe he loved Charlotte, then they deserved each other.

The twins weren't watching television.

Erin went from there to the bedrooms. Then she searched the house, but there were no twins. Finally she returned to the kitchen.

'They're not in the house,' she told Matt, and watched as his eyes widened. 'Where else could they be?'

'They're watching television.' He walked forward as if he thought she just wasn't looking hard enough, and flung open the sitting room door. The television was blaring, but there were no twins.

They looked at each other—and they started to run.

She checked the river first.

It was Erin's golden rule. Check out worst-case scenarios and work backward. The most dangerous places for the twins to be were the machinery shed and the river, so while Matt checked the sheds, she ran down along the track they'd used to go swimming.

They weren't there, but something else was there that made her suck in her breath in dismay.

Oh no!

She looked back up at the house, and her fears were confirmed. There was Matt, emerging from the shed where Cecil had been groomed. He was holding a twin by each hand. Erin couldn't see his face, but she could guess it'd look like thunder.

Because as soon as he saw the empty stall, he'd have guessed.

She turned around again and she sighed.

The river flowed on golden sand, and then curved away inland. As it did, the sand turned to mud.

That was where Cecil was. He was no longer confined, brushed and beautiful in the shed, ready for tomorrow's show. He was rolling full length in the mud, doing what every self-respecting bull would do, given all the peculiar odours they'd put on his body.

He was getting it all off.

And he was now disgusting!

CHAPTER SEVEN

'THEY deserve to be spanked. I'll do it if you won't.'
Charlotte was at her vitriolic best and Erin silently counted
to ten before she put herself between Charlotte and the
boys. Somehow she forced herself to think fast. She
needed a defensive weapon here, and luckily she had one,
just granted to her by an indignant Shanni.

'You touch them and I'll... I'll publish the poetry you
and Bradley Moore wrote to each other when you were
teenagers!'

What a threat! Erin's voice was whisper-quiet and desperate, but everyone knew she meant it. Matt's eyebrows
flew up in astonishment. Charlotte gasped and took a step
back, allowing Erin to crouch protectively before her two
white-faced little boys.

Now what? Erin thought desperately. The boys knew
exactly what they'd done, and how naughty they'd been.
Now they flinched, but they met her look, defiant and expecting the worst.

Why did she always want to hug them?

She couldn't. Matt was still holding them a hand apiece.
He was angry, she knew. He'd been distracted momentarily by her stupid threat to Charlotte, and she could see her
threat would surface to haunt her, but meanwhile he had
every right to be angry.

'What the...?' Charlotte was shocked to the core. 'You
never...'

'You used Rob McDonald as a go between,' Erin said,
and managed a smile. This was kids' poetry they were

talking about. It was only teasing, after all. Wasn't it? 'Silly move, Charlotte. Rob might be a police sergeant, but at fifteen he wasn't so law-abiding. The dratted boy copied them and Shanni found them a couple of weeks ago when she was cleaning up out at her parents' farm.'

It might be crazy, and wholly unethical, but as a desperate ruse it worked brilliantly. As a distraction, this was a beauty!

'That's ridiculous,' Charlotte managed, right off track.

'Yep!' It was, but Shanni had laughingly suggested it as a weapon, and it had been in Erin's head at the wrong time. Bay Beach was a very small town with a very long memory!

'Poetry,' Matt said blankly. *'Bradley?'* and Erin had to choke back laughter and concentrate on the important issue here.

'Do you know where Cecil is now?' she asked the boys gently. She was more dismayed than angry. Heaven, it was as if they tried to drive off anyone who was good to them. They'd all put in so much work to make Cecil splendid, and to undo it all now didn't make any sense. 'He's down in the mud by the river, and he's filthy,' she continued. 'All the work that you and Matt did is wasted.'

'We don't care,' William whispered.

'Now Matt won't be able to go to the show,' Henry added. He was scared stiff, but still there was a whisper of defiance. 'With her!'

And there was the crux of the matter. They wanted Matt to stay right here, so they'd taken matters into their own hands.

Help! Erin thought bleakly. They needed to be punished—but how? She couldn't let them off scot-free, and here was Charlotte ready to thrash them. All of them. Erin included.

The woman looked at explosion point. Maybe Erin's threat hadn't been such a good idea.

Concentrate on the twins, she told herself. 'You'd better go to your room,' she said wearily, trying to block out Charlotte's fury and think what was best. Her head was spinning. 'Oh, Matt, I'm so sorry.'

'There's no need for you to be sorry.' Matt's face was still grim, but there was a trace of understanding behind his eyes. Now they'd given their reason, he could see it and, damn, he'd had fun with the kids himself. He could see why they didn't want it to end. He hadn't thought it important—he'd assumed they'd be fine here with Erin while he was away for the night—but looking at it from a kid's perspective he could see where they were coming from.

And he could see the problem Erin had with them now. They needed consequences, but where were the consequences in this one? He stay home and they'd won? That'd achieve nothing except trouble next time. Or he'd work until midnight getting the bull ready again, and leave them all to be upset in his absence. Erin feeling guilty and the kids feeling bad.

Consequences...

Charlotte was quietly having kittens by his side. What had Erin said? Bradley Moore... Well, well.

Consequences!

'This is a real shame,' he said, and made himself look gravely at the twins instead of at Erin. He still had their hands. Now he gave them both a gentle tug so they were facing him. Unlike Erin, he didn't stoop. He stayed looking down at them from his great height, and he schooled his features into sad instead of angry.

Or...sadness instead of laughter?

'I can't believe you did this—just when I'd made the extra bookings,' he told them, and they stared.

'Bookings?' The twins knew they were expected to respond but they didn't know how. They didn't know what the word meant.

'For accommodation,' he told them. 'Since you'd done such a fine job helping me with Cecil, and since he needs a lot of grooming at the show, I'd decided you needed to come with me. I've just booked hotel rooms for you and Erin, so all of us could come.'

Erin blinked. Had he?

He hadn't. He'd only just thought of it, she decided as she watched his face, but it was a great idea. The boys faces dropped to their boots, and their look of incredulous disappointment was stunning.

'You were going to take us?' Henry whispered and Matt nodded.

'Yep. But it's no use now. We have a filthy bull.'

Charlotte's jaw had dropped in disbelief. 'You didn't...'

'Hush, Charlotte,' Matt told her kindly. Bradley Moore, eh? Brad was a bachelor farmer living not five miles away. The man was horse mad, and had the brains of a peanut.

But he couldn't think of that now.

'I guess none of us can go, now,' Matt said.

Silence. Erin was looking stunned, as well she might. She couldn't think of a better punishment for the boys than this if she'd thought for a week. To miss out on something as brilliant as the Lassendale show...

She felt a stab of disappointment herself, and had to remind herself that he'd only made it up to punish the boys.

'What if we catch him again?' Henry asked. 'We could wash him.'

Matt glanced at his watch. It was four-thirty already.

'I have things to do,' he said. 'A lot if I'm to get to the show. I haven't even started feeding yet.'

'If he's in the mud all by himself then we could catch him.' William was right there with Henry, and their two active little minds were in overdrive. 'If you gave us the rope...'

'And we can wash him. We know how to.'

'We helped the first time, and now we can do it ourselves.'

Erin compressed her lips, trying not to smile. Now what? Had Matt backed himself into a corner?

But no. He rose to the occasion with fortitude.

'I don't have the time to do it myself,' he told them. 'But if Erin's willing to supervise and you're willing to try—'

'They'll never do it,' Charlotte snapped, but Matt simply raised his eyebrows and smiled.

'They can try. I don't want to miss out on showing Cecil unless I must. He's a champion but I won't get the highest stud fees for him unless he's shown.'

'Can we try?' The twins were turning to Erin, their eyes a mixture of hope and despair. They knew they couldn't do it without her help, and they needed her.

So what was new? Kids always needed Erin.

And she was a farmer's daughter. Supervising the cleaning of one docile bull should be a piece of cake.

'You really have booked us accommodation?' she asked suspiciously. If she did let the boys go to this effort, Matt couldn't let them down at the end of it.

'I really have,' Matt told her. His eyes met hers and held, and something intangible passed between them. Some assurance that wasn't all about accommodation.

There was a moment's pause.

Then...

'What are we waiting for?' Erin asked. 'Come on, boys. Let's go find us a bull.'

And four hours later, once again they had a fine looking bull. Cecil was brushed and groomed to within an inch of his life, and the three of them had never worked so hard to make him that way. He was some bull, Erin thought. To have put up with it all twice in one day...

He had, and the boys had worked themselves to the point of exhaustion to make him perfect. They'd stopped briefly for dinner—sandwiches eaten on the back step so they wouldn't have to clean up—and then gone straight back to work until they'd finished. They gave Cecil the final brush-strokes right on eight, just as Matt strolled in for final inspection.

He'd kept far away from them all evening, knowing that was what was right, but it had cost him some resolution to do so. Charlotte had gone home an hour or more back, and it had been an almost superhuman struggle to stop his feet making their way to the shed.

Now though, it was all worthwhile as he entered to find three beaming faces, proudly displaying what they'd done.

And Cecil was practically beaming, too. He looked magnificent!

'What do you think?' Erin asked, and he heard the note of anxiety behind her words. She still thought that maybe he couldn't keep his word. That he'd say the bull wasn't good enough or there was a problem with accommodation.

But Matt was a man who was owed a few favours. As soon as Charlotte had gone he'd made some phone calls, and everything was set. Except Charlotte's temper, he thought ruefully. She'd slammed off home in a vile mood, and he could see all sorts of problems looming ahead.

Erin had overstepped the mark with her threat, but then,

he knew that Charlotte had been perfectly capable of slap-
ping the boys, and he also knew how urgent it had been
to stop her. She didn't understand what he instinctively
did—that a slap to kids who'd been kicked around in the
past meant the undoing of all of Erin's work.

So, in Matt's eyes, Erin was forgiven. And who couldn't
forgive her now? She was wet and mud-stained and there
was a soap bubble in her tangled curls that he just wanted
to reach out and...

'What do you think? she asked again, this time more
urgently, and he practically had to slap himself to get his
attention back where it was supposed to be.

Right. The bull. Cecil.

'I think our Cecil's never looked so good,' he told them,
and he included the boys in his broadest smile. 'Well done,
all of you.'

'Does that mean we can come to the show?' Henry demanded, and Matt nodded.

'Of course. I promised, didn't I?'

Yes, but they'd hardly believed him. William and Henry
exchanged significant glances and Erin could tell Matt had
gone up another notch in their estimation. Here was a
grown-up who meant what he said, and there hadn't been
too many of them in their lives. In their eyes Matt was
reaching hero proportions.

And in Erin's?

Cecil was quietly munching from his feed-box, and Erin
ran a hand down his glossy back, forcing herself to think
of practicalities rather than thinking of Matt. It was hard,
but necessary. Matt was engaged to Charlotte, she reminded herself bluntly and, even if he hadn't been, he was
way out of her league. Even if her errant heart was starting
to think otherwise.

It was just the way he smiled, she thought, and the way

he made her smile right back. His gentleness, and his intuitive knowledge of little boys…

Cut it out, she told herself harshly. There were still things that needed to be settled.

'I'll… I'll pay for us for the hotel accommodation,' she told him, but he shook his head.

'Nope. The boys worked hard for this. This is their payment.'

'But—'

He held up his hand. 'No buts. Just say thank you kindly, and go to bed.'

She grinned at that. 'Thank you kindly and go to bed,' she said, and the twins giggled.

It was a great sound. She looked down at their exhausted but happy faces, and she could have kissed the man who'd made this happen.

She darn near did—but she remembered all too well what had happened last time she'd tried something like that.

Once was enough.

Any more might be a disaster.

So at nine the next morning she was in the car, following the truck which was towing Cecil.

They had to go separately. The truck didn't fit five bodies and Erin's car wasn't strong enough to tow the trailer.

Charlotte's BMW could have done it, but Matt had enough sense not to suggest it. Charlotte was angry enough already, and to have the twins sitting on her gorgeous leather upholstery would be unthinkable. She hadn't suggested it herself, although he knew she didn't like travelling in his truck.

This way, though, she had Matt to herself and Erin was forced back into her place.

Behind her betters.

Which Erin didn't mind at all, she decided as she watched the trailer disappear around the first bend. They were moving fast. Let them go.

As the boys snoozed contentedly in the back, she turned the radio up and she sang along to schmaltzy songs at the top of her voice.

She was taking her boys to the Lassendale Show. They were happy, she was happy and not even Charlotte could spoil this one for her.

It was hard to say who was more impressed—Erin or the boys.

The show was an agricultural paradise. It lasted for two weeks. Matt had only come for the two days of Hereford judging and showing, but there were exhibitors there who'd camped the entire time.

As an exhibitor Matt had passes and he'd given one to Erin before he left. Therefore she parked her car easily enough, at the foot of the mountain that overlooked Lassendale, and then strolled with her two dumbstruck charges through the throng of people out to enjoy themselves.

Lassendale had started off a century before as a tiny country cattle show. Now, it was the biggest show in Australia, in the most gorgeous setting. The natural bushland had hardly been disturbed. Apart from the show ring and the cattle pavilions, the displays and side-shows were set up under clusters of spreading gums. Crowded or not, the place retained its natural beauty, and the sound of the distant sea could be heard whispering beneath the hubbub of the crowd.

Erin looked around her and felt a frisson of excitement building. It was gorgeous!

'We can afford to take our time,' she told the boys.

There were things here the boys would boggle at—amazing machinery, scary ghost rides and clowns where you poked ping pong balls into their mouths because 'every player wins a prize'.

Matt and Charlotte would already be here with Cecil, but they wouldn't need Erin or the twins. The judging was not for an hour. There were so many things to keep the boys entertained that she could take her time to find them.

But… 'We need to see Cecil straight away.' The boys were tugging her hands with urgency. 'What if Matt needs us to help? He might not get him looking beautiful in time. What if he lay down in the straw and messed his coat? And we want to see the judging. Erin, hurry.'

Erin grinned. They felt totally responsible for the bull, and she could only hope he didn't let them down when it came to judging time.

Not that it really mattered. If the judges didn't think Cecil was magnificent then the boys would simply decree him an idiot and do their own judging. In their eyes, Cecil was simply the best.

As was Matt, and Erin didn't take much persuading to turn her feet toward the cattle pavilion. Even if he was with Charlotte…

The boys were right. Cecil did look magnificent. Standing in his stall he seemed to have gained an aura of winner about him that hadn't existed at home.

'He's a born champion,' Matt told them as he stood back and admired his bull with pride. 'See how he holds his head? He never does that at home. He knows there are people looking at him, and it's all he can do not to preen.'

'Oh, for heaven's sake…' Charlotte had been jolted to bits in Matt's truck, she'd been stuck here for an hour while Matt groomed his precious bull and she wanted to be off to see the horses. But she couldn't go because Erin and the boys were coming, and some basic instinct told her she'd best stick around. But she didn't need to be gracious about it. 'The way you talk about him, you'd think he was intelligent!'

'You're saying my bull's not intelligent?' Matt teased her with his eyes but she didn't smile back. She wasn't in the mood for smiling.

'I know he's worth a fortune, but he's a bull, Matt.'

'Now you could put it much more diplomatically than that,' Erin told her, while the boys petted and fondled Cecil as if he was a very large and dopey dog rather than a pedigree bull. 'You could say you're sure he's almost as intelligent as his owner, and Matt would have to take it as a compliment.' Then, as Charlotte paused to work that one out, she scooped the boys back from the bull. 'Leave him be, boys. Matt has to take him through for judging now.'

'We want to watch.'

'It'll take an hour or so before we know the outcome,' Matt warned. 'The judges look at everything.'

'We'll wait,' Henry said firmly, and Matt and Erin exchanged looks. What harm could they get into? Matt's raised eyebrows asked, and Erin's imperceptible shake of her head told him she had the utmost faith in the boys to be on their best behaviour.

As they were.

No one was allowed near the cattle during judging. Only their owners stood by their side as the judges went over every inch of each beast.

Most family and friends took this time off to visit the fairgrounds—for something far more exciting than watching men watch cattle—but for all the interminable judging time the boys stood with bodies leaning over the fence that divided the public from the judging ring.

They were too far away to see what was happening, but it was as if they were willing Cecil to win, Erin thought as she watched their intent, silent faces. They watched and watched, as if part of themselves was being judged.

As indeed it was. They'd done the hard work. They'd paid their consequences, and when the blue ribbon was placed around Cecil's neck it was as much as Erin could do not to burst into tears at the look on their faces.

William did. He buried his face into Erin's breast and sobbed, while Henry just stood and stood, dumbstruck and silent.

'Well done, us,' Erin said in a voice that shook, gathering Henry into her as well as William. She found a tissue and mopped William's soggy face. 'Well done, all of us. And well done, Cecil.'

Then she looked up, and Matt was at the fence, leading Cecil away from the judges and beaming fit to bust. He'd seen them all. They'd been small figures in the distance, but he'd been so aware of them that the longing to win was no longer purely about what he could earn from his magnificent bull.

He knew how much the boys wanted this.

He'd wanted this ribbon for them—and for Erin.

He looked at her face, and he knew the trouble to get Cecil here—to get all of them here—had been worth it. She stood, her twins still tucked in beside her, and her eyes glowing with happiness. She was wearing Charlotte's sensible clothes—jeans and a checked shirt—and her normally unruly hair had been tied back in a sensible ponytail. She wore no make-up, but her face was lit with joy, and he wanted to hug her so badly…

Instead, he contented himself with hugging the twins,

grabbing them and swooping them over the fence, while Cecil looked on with placid bovine approval.

'This calls for a celebration,' he told them. He pushed a hand in his pocket and handed a note over to Erin. 'Here you go, cola and chips, fairy floss and a ride on the tunnel of death, courtesy of me.'

'Can we do that in reverse order?' Erin said faintly, thinking this through. 'Gee, Matt, thanks very much.'

'There's champagne for the grown-ups later,' he told her, and his smile was so warm she almost melted.

He was only being kind, she told herself sternly. Cut it out, Erin. Stop imagining things!

'We don't want to celebrate by ourselves,' Henry told him, casting a look for reassurance at his brother. 'Can you come with us?'

'I can't leave Cecil.' Matt's voice was sure, and Erin nodded. The farmers didn't leave their cattle. There were living facilities in the cattle pavilion. No one brought a bull as valuable as Cecil to a show and left him to the mercies of the general public. Even at the small shows around Bay Beach she'd learned that. No matter what they'd do tonight, Matt would be with his bull, sleeping on a camp stretcher beside him.

'Tell you what,' she told the twins. 'Why don't we go and buy a feast? A celebration feast. As much fairy floss, hot dogs, chips and fizzy drinks as we can find, and bring it back to share with Matt.'

Now it was Matt's turn to say, 'Gee, thanks,' and Erin's blue eyes danced.

'It'll be all our pleasure. Is there anything you'd like to add to our list?'

He thought about it. Fairy floss, huh. 'A beer would do nicely.' Before or after fairy floss? Good grief!

'Coming right up,' she sang, and they trooped away, leaving Matt and Cecil staring after them.

'She's quite a girl,' he told Cecil, and Cecil pushed his great head against Matt's chest, and nudged him sideways, as if reminding him of his duties.

He got the point. 'You're right. I have a woman. I'm an engaged man.' Matt shook his head as if dispelling a dream. He looked down at his bull and he grinned. 'Not like you. You can have thousands of them. In the human world we're restricted to one, and a very suitable one she is, too.'

Charlotte had gone to inspect the horses, and he badly wanted her here now, to see Cecil's ribbon and to share the moment.

Or maybe he didn't.

Maybe it was enough that Erin had seen it and was coming back to celebrate.

'Where are you going to sleep?'

It had turned into a party. The twins were working their way through mountains of junk food, Erin had had the forethought not to bring back one beer but a crate of two dozen, and half the cattle pavilion seemed to be crowded into Cecil's stall.

Not Charlotte, though. She was off doing her own thing.

Which was how it should be, Matt thought doubtfully as Henry questioned his sleeping arrangements. That was why he'd decided she'd be a suitable wife. She'd lead her own life and he'd lead his...

But it was sort of nice being surrounded by kids—and by Erin.

'Where are you sleeping?' Henry's small hand was in his, clutching him urgently as he repeated his question. 'Erin says we're staying in a hotel but you're not.'

'I'm staying here.'

'Where?'

His eyes met Erin's for a fleeting moment over Henry's head. She was laughing at something one of the cattlemen had said, but he knew by the sudden stillness of her body that she'd heard what was being said, and was gently mocking him. See if you can stay uninvolved, her body language said, and for the life of him he couldn't.

'Matt gets to sleep in the nice comfy straw with Cecil and all these great people and these wonderful animals,' she told Henry, making her voice mournful. 'While poor old us get to sleep between sheets in a really comfortable hotel.'

Silence while the twins took this on board. Then came the inevitable—'We want to sleep on the straw, too,' Henry said.

'Yes,' said William.

It would be sort of fun, Erin thought. Staying here with these down-to-earth farmers instead of going back to the hotel, putting the boys to sleep and then spending the evening with Charlotte.

No! Spending the evening alone!

'Matt's booked us into a really great hotel,' she told the kids. 'With a swimming pool.'

'It'd be better here. We don't want a swimming pool. Matt's river's better.'

'Yes, but we don't have sleeping bags—and I'll bet Matt's already paid a deposit for the hotel.' She was all with the kids on this one, but it wouldn't work. Even if their sleeping bags hadn't been burned in the fire, which they had, sleeping in the cattle pavilion—with Matt—was probably unwise. In more ways than one.

But bad news had a habit of travelling fast in country communities. Even though they were now a hundred miles from Bay Beach, most of the people in the pavilion knew exactly who Erin and her boys were. They were receiving sympathy from all sides, and they received more now.

'Bet your sleeping bags and stuff were burned in the fire,' the cattleman she'd been talking to growled, and when she nodded he chewed his bottom lip.

'There you go then, boys,' he said to the cattle shed in general. 'Kids and the lady want to stay here. We've been thinking of a way we could help and here it is.' He hauled his hat from his head and tossed a twenty dollar bill into it. 'Here's a start.' He passed the disreputable Akubra on to his neighbour.

'This is a whip round, and when we have enough my Bert'll go downtown and fetch what you need. Three full swags with our compliments. No arguments, girl. The hotel room Matt's booked will be snatched up by any of a score of people who need accommodation and who don't figure, like us, that the place we have here is fit for kings. And as for the swags... It'll be our pleasure to buy them for you.'

The generosity was immediate and almost overwhelming. It left Erin with nothing to say but thank you. Despite Erin's protestations, there was no resisting the wave of generosity passing through the shed, and the hat with the money disappeared out the door before she could see it.

Bert returned half an hour later, laden with swags—padded sleeping mats, sleeping bags, mosquito nets and pillows. Following him in was Charlotte, and, to Erin's surprise, she appeared delighted with the new sleeping arrangements.

'That's wonderful,' she told a bemused Matt, tucking a proprietorial arm through his. 'It means Erin can stay here and look after your beastly bull and you can stay at the hotel with me.'

There would now be a free room, Erin thought, and then thought, they're engaged, why would Matt even need a spare room? The thought, for some stupid reason, made her feel ill.

It didn't suit the twins, either. They'd been checking out the sleeping bags with whoops of delight, but now they paused, mid whoop.

'Matt's sleeping with us,' William said uncertainly and Henry stuck his thumb in his mouth in affirmation. The little boy looked up at Charlotte as if she was some slug-like creature who even his small boy's interest in slug-like creatures would still find repelling.

For once, Erin was in sympathy with his sentiments entirely.

But she couldn't admit it.

'Of course Matt can stay with Charlotte,' she made herself say. 'It makes sense.'

'Of course it makes sense,' Charlotte snapped, resentful that Erin felt she had any influence at all on Matt's sleeping arrangements.

But Matt had other ideas. He knew by now exactly what the twins were capable of. Not that they'd worry Cecil, he thought. He knew them well enough by now to accept that if he told them they were guarding Cecil then they'd do it as if their lives depended on it, but what else they might do...

No! Erin's job was to look after her twins, and his job was to look after Cecil. He couldn't ask her to do both.

'I'm sleeping here,' he told Charlotte and watched her face darken. Damn, now he had to feel guilty!

'Don't you trust me with your bull?' Erin teased, and he cast her an exasperated glance.

'You have enough on your hands.'

'I normally look after five kids,' she told him, and her

eyes were still teasing. Damn, they had the ability to mes-
merise a man. 'Two kids and a bull should be a piece of
cake.'

'Erin…'

'Darling, don't be stupid.' Charlotte's hand was still
resting on his arm and he had to fight back the urge to
shake it off. 'You know you can come.'

'Do you know how much this bull's worth?' he demanded, driving her against the ropes. If there was one
thing Charlotte understood it was money.

'But Matt…'

He didn't trust them completely, Erin thought, watching
the affianced couple, and who could blame him? If it was
her priceless bull, would she leave him with the twins?

Yes, but then she knew her twins!

'Look, let's compromise,' Erin suggested. Goodness,
here she went again. This was what being a House Mother
was all about—finding compromises before there was a
scene, and the cattlemen listening around them meant that
a scene would be quite spectacular.

'Matt, what if you take Charlotte out for dinner while
we care for Cecil? Then you can come back here to sleep.
I guess we'll probably be dead to the world by the time
you return, but we'll set up our bags right by Cecil and
we promise we won't leave him alone for a moment. He'll
be safe—won't he boys?'

'Yes,' said William, and Henry took his thumb from his
mouth long enough to say,

'Yes, if he really has to go out with *her*…'

'He really does. Don't you, Matt?'

And, with the eyes of the entire pavilion on him, what
was a man to do but agree?

CHAPTER EIGHT

As RESTAURANTS went, Charlotte would have rated this one as entirely satisfactory.

Show time was Lassendale's biggest two weeks of the year. The hotel Charlotte was staying in was five star, and the restaurant chefs had pulled out all the stops to impress a clientele which, for these two weeks, was international and wealthy. Therefore Matt—who'd packed a suit as he always did, for business meetings with those who were interested in what Cecil could provide—escorted Charlotte into the dim recesses of the dining room and he knew he was in for a gastronomical treat.

He wasn't disappointed. The waiter took one look at the sleek and svelte Charlotte and her handsome companion, and he ushered them to the best table, gave them the best service and they were treated to the best food Lassendale could offer.

Matt had an appetiser of some sort of tiny goat's cheese souffle. Entrée was ginger chilli prawns cooked to perfection, and then steak...

Steak!

Cecil.

Matt found his thoughts wandering right back to his bull—and to the people who'd be guarding him. All through appetiser and entrée he'd fought to keep his attention on Charlotte's small talk, but he could ignore the pull of his conscience no longer.

'Maybe we should give sweets a miss,' he told Charlotte tensely. 'I'm a bit unhappy about Cecil.'

He wasn't. He just...

He just didn't know, but it didn't seem right that Erin was back there and he was here.

'Oh, for heaven's sake!' Charlotte gave a soft laugh and put her hand over his. Curiously the motion made him flinch. It was all he could do not to pull away, and the sensation was starting to worry him. This was the woman he intended marrying, he told himself. To flinch was ridiculous.

He forced himself to return the pressure of her hand as she continued.

'Darling, Erin does come from solid farming stock. I remember she used to take her father's herd droving through the drought years when she was little more than a child herself. My parents were horrified, but I gather she coped very well.'

She had, too, Matt thought. Droving... He'd forgotten that.

Matt let Charlotte chatter on, but his thoughts flew elsewhere. In his late teens there'd been a drought which had left every farm in the district low on feed. Farms like Matt's and Charlotte's, where there'd been money to spare, had brought in food from interstate. But the Douglas family hadn't been in that position and Jack Douglas, bereft from the loss of his children's mother, simply didn't care.

That had been the end of Erin's formal schooling, he remembered. With seven siblings to feed and clothe, she couldn't afford to let the farm go under. Aged all of fifteen years old, she'd taken herself out of school and driven her cattle around the dusty district roads, letting them graze on any roadside where there'd been any growth at all.

It was a desperate measure to keep her breeding stock alive. Somehow she'd managed it, and managed it alone, though he still didn't know how.

And he remembered his mother's fury when she discovered his father had taken Erin a pile of hay to let her stay in the same place for a while.

'If the drought keeps up much longer we'll need it ourselves,' she'd hissed. 'You don't have to feel sorry for every destitute little tramp in the district...'

Destitute little tramp...

He looked into Charlotte's flushed face and he knew she'd felt exactly the same. Erin had been very much alone then, and she was very much alone now.

'I'll go back,' he said flatly, and the hand in his suddenly stilled.

'Matt, don't be stupid. I'd like sweets, and there's dancing afterwards.'

'But I have responsibilities.' And then he looked up as a man he recognised appeared in the entrance. Bradley Moore. Of course. Bradley always stayed in the finest establishment, and he was always looking for someone to talk with about his horses. Charlotte was just the woman. She even liked horses! He lifted an arm. 'Hi, Bradley. Over here!'

'Matt!'

'You like Bradley, don't you?'

To his amazement, Charlotte blushed from the tip of her manicured toenails to the roots of her sleekly chignoned hair. 'Yes, but...'

'There you go, then,' he said amiably. Why had he never seen how suited these two were? 'Bradley, I need to go back to my bull. Could you keep Charlotte entertained on my behalf?'

'Why...' Bradley, the sort of half-wit who couldn't decide whether to look like a Really Important Person or a half-baked kipper, looked stunned but incredulously delighted. 'Of course.'

'Of course.' Matt beamed. 'I'll leave you be, then. Will you come out and watch Cecil in the grand parade tomorrow, Charlotte?'

'I might,' she said peevishly. She was seriously annoyed. 'It depends on what Bradley's doing.'

'Right ho,' said Matt, with all the amiability in the world, and made his escape.

They hadn't missed him a bit. That much was clear the moment he walked into the cattle pavilion.

While he'd been wining and dining Charlotte, the cattlemen had set up a barbecue. The aroma of seared sausages and steak hit him the moment he entered the doors, and he thought fleeting of the grossly overpriced steak back at the hotel and wondered how much better it had been.

A hundred bucks better? he wondered, and he knew darned well it wasn't.

He'd missed out on sweets back at the hotel, but he needn't have worried. The moment he was sighted, he was handed a plate of pavlova.

'Get that into you, Matt McKay,' a cheerful young matron told him. 'You almost missed out. And then get into a set. Your family have been at it an hour or more, and if you don't join in soon they'll have danced their legs off without you.'

His family...

It was the strangest feeling, but that was exactly how it felt. He stood on the sidelines absently spooning in pavlova—which was a shame because the crisp meringue and the gorgeous sun-ripened strawberries deserved all his attention—and he watched his 'family' dance.

'Swing your partners, round we go.'

The square dancing was at a frantic pace. One of the

cattlemen had produced a fiddle, another a mouth organ, and the centre of the pavilion had been cleared for the dancers. Now it was a mass of whirling, laughing, cattlemen and women, teenagers, kids and even the odd dog.

And Erin and her twins were in the middle of everything. They were part of a set, the twins were obeying the caller's instructions as if their lives depended on it, and Erin…

Erin was being swung from one appreciative cattleman to another. And what she was wearing…

It was the new dress she'd bought in town with Shanni and it was gorgeous! All the colours of the rainbow, with a full circle skirt that flew out like a whirling, flaming hoop around her, it was a dress that had to be seen to be believed. Her hair was flying free, her gorgeous blue eyes were sparkling with laughter and her face was flushed with exertion.

She looked so desirable that it almost killed Matt to stay on the sidelines and eat his pavlova. But to join the set you needed a partner, and there were no spare women. Except…

Except the pavlova lady who'd just handed over her last piece of pavlova. With a whoop of triumph, Matt cast off his coat and tie, seized the unsuspecting lady and whirled her onto the dance floor before she had time to object.

Now it was just a matter of working his way up the line to Erin…

'Hey, William, Matt's here!' Henry was doing his darnedest to whirl around a very fat lady of advancing years—and not doing such a bad job of it either. The lady was whirling as required, though Henry, trying valiantly to clutch her around the waist, merely had an armful of thigh, and her breast was threatening to crush him at any moment.

William was doing better. He was paired at the moment with a young lady not much older—or bigger—than he was, but the responsibility of the occasion didn't give him time to respond. There was a twirly bit coming up and he had to get it right....

But Erin had heard.

'Matt!' She was flying past him as she threaded in and out of the dancers. Darn! Matt hadn't realised this wasn't a 'change your partners' set. She was threading and so was a stud of a cattleman who he didn't recognise but disliked on sight. 'What have you done with Charlotte?' she called, and he dredged up a smile.

'Left her with Bradley.'

Her eyebrows hit the roof. She gave that delicious chuckle and then someone else swung her away, she flew back to the arms of her cattleman and she was lost to him.

There was no more contact then for about five minutes, until it was time for Matt and his partner to take their turn threading to the lead. Then, as he whirled Erin around to change to the other side of the set, she laughed up into his face.

'You must have the utmost faith in her,' she teased, and he glowered.

'Why wouldn't I?'

'With your bank balance?' Still she was laughing. 'No, indeed.'

And then Erin was gone, leaving him to glower some more and then regain his composure as he joined his partner again and found she was looking up at him in mute enquiry.

She really was bouncy and pretty herself, he told himself. The twins were having the time of their lives and the whole pavilion was having fun. Even the cattle were watching with bovine approval.

There was no earthly reason—or even a logical one—
for a man to sulk just because Erin was dancing with someone else. He gave himself a huge mental shrug and decided
to have fun.

Which he did.

They danced on. The music went on into the night. The
twins decided it was more fun whooping around the cattle
stalls with other kids than being squeezed from bosom to
bosom. The cattlemen ended up with their wives or lovers.
And Matt...

Matt finally ended up with Erin. They danced on. The
music slowed, and maybe he should have stopped, but Erin
felt sort of nice, with her hands in his, then sort of closer,
her breasts against his chest, his mouth nuzzling her soft
curls, the scent of some faint perfume drifting upward and
making him feel...

That was enough of that! Enough! This was tantalising,
unwise, unplanned, thoughtless, and hopeless.

The music stopped as the musicians finally ran out of
puff, and Erin and Matt were left looking at each other in
the middle of the dance floor-cum-cattle shed. They were
still holding each other. Still sort of feeling...

They had twins!

As the music stopped, the kids in the pavilion returned
reluctantly to their respective parents. Most were heading
off with one or both parents to a hotel, but a few were
camping with the cattle tenders, as Matt and Erin were.

'It's time to go to bed,' William announced importantly
for what must surely be the first time in his life he had
ever asked voluntarily to go to bed. He was head-butting
Erin's thigh to get her attention. Totally unaware of the
currents of sexual awareness between the two adults, he
was onto the next thing on the twins' agenda. Which was
sleeping in the straw.

'We need to set up our beds,' Henry told them, and reluctantly, Erin's hands were released and the twins were included in between them. There was a sandwich of adults with kid filling, and the frisson of warmth and linkage remained the same. It felt so right!

'So we do,' Matt said, but his eyes were still on Erin. There were matters here that were unresolved.

And that had to remain unresolved, he thought fiercely, forcing himself to remember Charlotte back at the hotel and all the logical reasons why he'd decided to marry her. Charlotte was a sensible choice, he told himself harshly. Good grief! If he married because of a spur-of-the-moment attraction, he could have married fifteen years ago, and where would he be now? Burdened with school fees, chaos, change to his mother's lovely, ordered house...

Marry with your head, not your heart, his mother had said over and over, until it had become almost a mantra.

There was more of his mother in him than he thought, he decided ruefully. Fifty-fifty gene split? Yeah, there he had it. He was half his father who loved the farm and didn't mind a little chaos occasionally, and half his mother who liked order and beauty and...

'Hey, Matt, we're just organising somewhere to sleep.' Erin's voice was chiding him gently, and her blue eyes were full of laughter. She could see exactly what he was thinking! Damn her!

'Do you think we'll all fit in with Cecil?' William was asking anxiously, and somehow Matt tore his mind from where it definitely wanted to go and forced himself to think of sleeping arrangements.

And there were dangers there, too.

'Of course we'll fit,' Erin said soundly. 'We just have to persuade Cecil to move to the back of his stall.'

Hmm. Easier said than done.

The stalls weren't huge, but they were all the space al-
located to them which was why at most, one or two people
were bedding down beside each animal. If Cecil lay width-
ways at the back of the stall the thing was possible, but if
he'd done that his rear would be against one wooden di-
vision and his nose would be pressed against the other.
Cecil was nothing if not large!

So Cecil, being the sensible animal he was, was lying
full length on the hay, his nose poking out onto the walk-
way so he could gaze his fill at the dancers. He was one
sleepy bovine, and he looked as if his intentions to shift
were at about nil.

'I suppose if we all shoved,' Erin said doubtfully and
Matt grimaced.

'Yep. You and a two-ton crane might do it.'

Which left two strips of hay three feet wide on either
side of Cecil, stretching back the eight feet or so to the
rear of the stall.

'We can take a twin each and sleep on either side,' Matt
said slowly. But it wasn't the arrangement his gut
wanted—and he might have known it didn't suit the twins
either.

'We want to sleep together.' Of course.

'You will be sleeping together,' Matt told them without
much hope of being heard. 'Except instead of a pillow
between you there'll be Cecil.'

'We can't share Tigger. And Cecil's as big as a mountain.' Henry put a finger on his nose. 'See? He's up to
here.'

Erin choked, and Matt frowned her down. Didn't the
woman realise there was no alternative?

Apparently she didn't.

'Of course you must sleep together,' she told them. 'You
can't cut Tigger in half. So, into the bathroom, into your

pyjamas and then into these wonderful sleeping bags. Now!' It was her command voice and the boys responded accordingly.

'Okay.' They hesitated just long enough for William to ask; 'But where will you sleep?'

'Matt and I will top and tail on the other side, of course,' she said—as if the matter had never been in doubt.

'Top and tail?' Matt was frowning and she grinned.

'Easy to see you haven't slept in a family with eight children,' she told him. 'You fit two in a bed this way, and it minimises fights. It doesn't stop them entirely—' another grin '—but I'm sure we can fight quietly. You sleep with your head near Cecil's head and I sleep with my head near Cecil's butt. We'll be cosy as two bugs in a rug. The only thing is...' She looked down at her toes and grimaced.

'Yes?' he said resignedly. This woman was nuts. Nice, but definitely nuts!

'After all that dancing and carting cattle around all day, maybe you'd better not take your boots off, Mr McKay. If there's one thing I can't bear sleeping with, it's a man with stinking socks!'

Matt's socks weren't the problem.

There wasn't room for Matt's camp bed or Erin's blow-up mattress—not both—but the hay was thick and fresh. Matt hauled his sleeping bag up to his chin, tossed his pillow beside Cecil's head and lay down. Erin did the same, lying in reverse, but nobly Matt had left her the side against the wood partition.

On the other side of Cecil, the twins snuggled in with plenty of room. Their noses barely reached Cecil's neck, and their toes didn't reach his rear end. Once assured Erin and Matt were settled for the night right on the other side

of Cecil, they closed their eyes on their shared pillow,
snuggled Tigger and were out for the count. Two exhausted but perfectly content children.

As Erin was content. Matt's legs were distracting, and
she was absurdly aware of the presence of his body so
close to her, but this was a way of sleeping she'd been
brought up with. She could cope.

'Erin?' It was a hoarse whisper and Matt's toes nudged
her shoulder to gain her attention. He had it!

'Yep?' She had to whisper back. The entire pavilion was
settled to sleep now, and the lights had been turned low.
Cattle and cattle carers alike were purposefully sleeping.

Not Matt. 'Erin, Cecil's chewing.'

She choked on a bubble of laughter. 'He's what?'

'He's chewing.'

She thought about that, and nodded into the dimness. 'I
wouldn't worry. Cattle do.'

'Not right in my ear, they don't.'

'Take away his feed, then.' Honestly!

'He's not chewing his feed,' Matt told her, and there
was a trace of desperation in his whisper. 'At a guess, he's
chewing yesterday's feed, or even...' His toes nudged her
shoulder again as if to emphasise the awfulness of it. 'By
the smell of it, even the day before's!'

'Are you saying,' Erin asked, trying not to laugh out
loud, 'that your champion bull has halitosis?'

'If halitosis means breath that stinks like rancid garlic,
then yes,' Matt told her, forgetting to whisper and being
shushed from about six different stalls for his pains.
'That's exactly what I'm saying. And he keeps trying to
lick my face.'

'He loves you.'

'Oh, right.'

'You want to swap sides so I'm against Cecil?'

'All that means is that he'll lean over your feet to lick my face.'

'So...'

'So I'm shifting!' Matt was nothing if not a man of decision, and some decisions were easy. Cecil or Erin? Erin won every time. He rose, sleeping bag and all, hopped until his feet were with Erin's and then flopped down again onto the straw.

Which meant that now his face was level with Cecil's tail. And Erin's nose.

There was no room for two pillows. They had to share.

Uh, oh... Maybe this hadn't been such a good idea after all.

The intimacy which had been building during the night had dispersed a little while putting the twins to bed and settling themselves. Now however it slammed back like a lightning bolt. Unconsciously Erin found herself hauling her sleeping bag zipper higher, right to her chin. As if that could protect her from what she was feeling...

'Hey, I'm not into seduction mode here,' Matt told her, seeing her movement and trying to make light of it. 'It's just if I have a choice of being kissed by you or by Cecil...'

Being kissed?

He'd meant to say licked!

No. That wasn't right either. Hell, his whole body was going rigid with the strain of having her so close.

'You prefer me to Cecil?' Like Matt, Erin was trying desperately to keep things light. She chuckled and rolled over to face him—which was another mistake as she hadn't realised how close he was. His nose was inches from hers. Major mistake!

'You...' Her voice cracked and it was only after a couple of desperate swallows that she made it work again. 'You mean it? Matt, it's the very sweetest thing to say, but I'm very sure you don't mean it. One of the guys I was dancing with tonight told me what Cecil is worth. That'd make ten of me and then some.'

Maybe.

'But only one of Charlotte,' she teased gently. 'She's a lady who knows her worth.'

'She is...special,' Matt said grudgingly and tried like crazy to conjure up Charlotte's image. The image refused to be conjured. All he could see was a smattering of freckles, one pert nose and gorgeous, laughing eyes. And lips that were so soft...

Hell!

'She's a lucky lady, too,' Erin whispered warmly into the dark, seemingly unaware of the sensations he was feeling. 'To be marrying you. You're one fantastic guy, Matt McKay. To have given the twins today... It was just great.'

'And it'll stay great as long as Cecil doesn't roll over and squash the pair of them.'

He must stop looking at her lips. He must!

'As if he would,' Erin said indignantly. 'As well as expensive, he's also intelligent.'

'He is at that.'

And it was the truth. Matt's pride in his bull was almost overwhelming. Cecil was the result of years and years of careful planning and selective breeding. Up until now, he'd been Matt's pride and joy. He still was! But up until now, Cecil was the first thing he thought of when he woke in the morning, and his last thought as he slept at night.

And if he'd had to choose between Cecil and Charlotte, the choice would be obvious and absolute.

Cecil or Erin, though....

No! This was ridiculous. He liked a simple and ordered existence, he thought desperately. He wanted an existence where he farmed and Charlotte kept the house and his social life nicely ordered.

That was how he'd been raised, with his mother and father living together but in separate worlds, and that was the way he believed the world worked. As it would continue to work.

Except…there was this woman right before his nose!

But this woman came with complications, and they weren't just minor hiccups. They were major. She came with a pair of troubled twins, and he just knew wherever Erin went it wouldn't be just the twins that'd follow.

Get involved with Erin Douglas and he knew there'd be more kids, his and others, every lame duck in the district, every hard luck story…

And the boundaries between house and farm would cease to exist. He knew it. There'd be a riot of kids and dogs inside and out, and Erin herself wouldn't know her place. She'd be out heaving hay or grooming cows or…or somewhere he couldn't get away from her.

Like now. He was trapped two inches from her cute nose, and hell, all he wanted to do was kiss her.

'Would you stop looking at me like a rabbit caught in a floodlight?' she said suddenly, and there was no way he could escape the gentle mockery in her tone. Could she really know what he was thinking?

Apparently, yes. 'Matt McKay, you are very, very cute, but you are an engaged person and I am not the least bit interested. I take the lust I'm looking at in your eyes right now as a compliment, I am exceedingly grateful for all you've done for me and the twins but I want nothing more from you than enough space to go to sleep. So you can stop looking at me like I'm going to lunge at your body any minute and you can go to sleep. Now!'

'Hey, I'm not expecting anything!'

'And neither am I,' she said firmly. 'So there's nothing to stop either of us from sleeping.' And without another word she rolled over and put her face to the wall.

He rolled over, too, which left his nose pressed against Cecil's butt. The comparison to what he'd just been looking at was ridiculous.

And her butt was against his. There was simply no room for it not to be.

Sleep? Ha! All he could feel was her. All he could think of was her. She was so…

So right out of his league! In every single way he could think of.

As for Erin? She'd said she was going to sleep, but it wasn't quite that easy. He was too darned close. Too darned male.

Too…too everything!

'I am not interested in Matt McKay,' she told herself fiercely. Not. Not. Not!

But he was the most gorgeous male she'd ever slept with in her life! That wasn't saying much, she thought ruefully. Erin had always been so involved with her kids that men usually ran a mile, sensing that commitment with Erin meant commitment to a whole lot more.

But Matt was certainly gorgeous.

And he was so darned nice! He was so nice that she wanted to turn right over and…

'That's enough of that,' she whispered into the dark. 'Go to sleep!'

CHAPTER NINE

ERIN slept late. Late, that is, in cattle terms. It must have been three a.m. or later before she'd finally fallen into an uneasy slumber, she was dog tired and she was accustomed to noise. So maybe it wasn't surprising that when she finally woke, the rest of the cattle pavilion was bustling.

As were Matt and the twins. Erin rolled sleepily over and found herself looking at ten legs. Four belonged to Cecil who was standing looking regally around as his minions worked over him. Four belonged to the twins, who, armed with a brush apiece, were intent on making Cecil look even more regal.

And two belonged to Matt.

'Well, well. Sleepy-head's finally decided to grace us with her consciousness. Good morning, Miss Douglas.'

'Good...good morning.' She brushed the sleep from her eyes and sat up, then gasped and hauled her sleeping bag up to her neck. She must have pulled the zipper down in her sleep, and her nightdress wasn't exactly decent...

'Have a coat,' Matt said, and tossed a waterproof down to her, though by the glint in his eyes she knew he'd seen—and approved of what he'd seen. 'Bathroom's that-way, lady, but you'd better scuttle or you'll miss breakfast.'

'Breakfast?' She was still befuddled by sleep and totally bewildered.

'Pancakes at two o'clock,' he told her, doing a sweeping circle of the pavilion until he was pointing to a barbecue at the far end. 'Courtesy of the Country Women's

Association. But the dress code's a bit rigid. Nightgowns with unfastened buttons don't reach their standards.'

She gasped. Enough!

She clutched his waterproof to her while awkwardly escaping from her sleeping bag, then bolted, tinglingly aware that his eyes stayed on her until the door closed behind her.

It was a silly, happy, busy couple of hours before the Grand Parade.

Breakfast was delicious—steak and sausages for those with strong constitutions, but pancakes and honey for those with a bit more finesse. 'Which is me,' Erin declared, watching Matt chomp into his beef. 'And in front of Cecil, too. Honestly, Matt, have you no sensitivity?'

'If you think for one minute that Cecil will end up as beef steak...'

'His cousins might.'

'They'd have to be pretty inferior cousins.'

'I don't care. I'm sticking to pancakes. What about you boys?' And although the twins desperately wanted to be like Matt, honesty prevailed and pancakes won the day.

'Weaklings,' Matt declared but the boys looked up into his twinkling eyes and knew he was kidding them.

Honestly, Erin thought. For a man to get away with calling the twins weaklings—and for the twins to love it..

She could seriously fall for this man—if he wasn't already spoken for. Or if he wasn't rich. Or... If a million other things that weren't going to happen!

Breakfast finished, the whole pavilion settled down to the serious business of making their animal the most magnificent. The animals left here now were all winners, but none looked as great as Cecil, Erin thought, but she knew she was biased. The four of them worked as a team, going way past the necessary preparations for a bull who'd already won champion of his class.

'Do you think I should tie a big blue bow around his ears?' she asked as she stood back and admired their handiwork. 'And maybe a matching one on his tail?'

'Over my dead body.' Matt stood beside her and grinned. 'I'll have you know my bull's a he-man and I want him to stay that way. His testosterone level would plummet at the first bow.'

'And that would never do,' she said mockingly. 'A McKay male with suspect testosterone...'

'We try to keep it above the run of the herd,' Matt said smugly.

'Brains or balls.' Erin nodded sagely as she gazed at Cecil's amazing appendages. 'Yep, I can see the choice has been made here.' Then, as Matt drew in his breath, she took a wise step away from him. 'Come on, twins,' she said, choking back laughter at the expression on Matt's face. 'There's no way you can get Cecil more beautiful than he is right now. It's time for Matt to take him out.'

'Wait a bit.' Matt had control of himself now—almost—and he was thinking. He was enjoying himself enormously, he thought, and the realisation was hitting home that his enjoyment was coming to an end.

It shouldn't be. The Grand Parade here was the ultimate achievement. Already he'd had a steady stream of potential customers, national and international, pass by Cecil's stall and assess for themselves his stud potential. In the parade, they'd be watching from the stands, making their final decision on which stud farm to choose.

Cecil moved magnificently. In the stalls he looked great, but out in the open he swayed with a majesty that had to be seen to be believed. For potential customers interested in Herefords there was now no choice, Matt knew, and he also knew his income for the next twelve months would skyrocket.

So, for Matt, the parade was the culmination of years of hard work. This was what he, his father and his grandfather had spent years achieving.

Why then, did he feel reluctant to take the rope attached to Cecil's halter and tug the giant beast toward the parade ring?

Because this year showing Cecil and winning first prize wasn't the highlight, he thought suddenly. It was working side by side with others; with this funny, warm and lovely woman and her two troubled charges.

This was pure novelty factor, he thought harshly, trying to bring himself back down to earth. He had no intention of working side by side with a woman. He worked alone. That was the way he'd been brought up. It was the order of things, now and forever...

'Matt! Oh, darling, he's wonderful!'

It was almost a relief to look up and see Charlotte bearing down on them—a Charlotte refreshed by a good night's sleep in the hotel, and wearing her signature apparel of white on white. White slacks. White linen blouse with collar that just stood up the right amount. A white on white silk scarf, casually knotted. The very epitome of casual elegance in a wealthy farmer's wife.

She didn't have straw sticking out of her hair like Erin did. She hadn't stepped in a cow pat in her only pair of shoes, forcing her to wear borrowed gum boots three sizes too big—as Erin had.

She was a much more suitable woman, Matt told himself.

The trouble was, she might be more suitable, but she wasn't nearly as much fun.

Life wasn't fun, he told himself. Hadn't his parents

taught him anything? Work wasn't fun. Fun was some-thing you had intermittently with your mates, when the women weren't around. Fun was…

Hell, he didn't know what fun was any more.

Wasn't fun what they'd had this morning?

'He's a fine-looking beast.' With a jolt, Matt hauled himself out of his strange line of thought and realised Charlotte wasn't alone. Bradley was right behind her, his portentous tones echoing through the pavilion. 'I hope you don't mind me escorting Charlotte back here?'

Yep, the weed still remembered the drubbing Matt had given him at school when he'd paraded his self-importance from age ten, and he wasn't risking anything here.

'But when I found Charlotte had no one to drive her…'

'You brought her from the hotel. Very kind.' Matt was suddenly feeling almost overwhelmingly claustrophobic. 'I'm sorry, Charlotte. I have to go. Cecil's required in the ring. Bradley, could you look after Charlotte for me?'

'Creighton Bow is also required in the ring,' Bradley said stiffly. 'The horses come in straight after cattle. My lads are grooming him for me now.'

'Creighton Bow.' Oh, right. Bradley's wonderful horse. 'Um…right. Did he win, then?'

'He gained a second placing. I felt the judging over-looked—'

'I'll look out for him,' Matt said hastily. 'Well done.' But inside he was cringing in repugnance. To let his lads groom what he knew was a magnificent stallion, without even supervision… To stay the night in the hotel while his precious bloodstock was here… The claustrophobia was rising by the minute.

'I need to go.'

But then there were two urgent little hands tugging his

shirt. 'Can we come, too? Please, Matt? Can we come, too?'

Matt hesitated—and was lost. A thought hit him, and it was as if a thunderbolt had crashed into his solar plexus. Good grief!

'Matt, please...'

Why not?

He'd seen this happen. Livestock had been led into the ring by youngsters before, and he'd always thought, how the hell could you put all that work into breeding and preparing an animal and then let someone else show it?

It was like Bradley letting someone else groom his horse.

But it wasn't like that, he realised suddenly. Bradley let someone else do the hard work and then would take the glory himself. He'd lead Creighton Bow into the ring. Matt looked down into the two desperately eager little faces and he knew that if he let his bolt of lightning idea have its way he'd have two levels of pride. Not one.

He'd never seen it before, but there it was. All those years of watching kids...

His father would never have dreamed of such a thing, he thought, and if he did his mother wouldn't have allowed it.

But he wasn't his father, and the idea was like slicing the past from the future. He cast an uncertain glance at Erin, unsure how she'd react, but there was no chance of taking her aside and sounding his idea out.

She looked ridiculous, he thought. She looked unkempt, frazzled, over-booted and underdressed beside Charlotte's perfect dress code, but his lips twitched at the sight of her and it was only with difficulty that he turned his attention back to the twins.

They were waiting to be turned down. He could see by

their eyes that they'd asked to come, too, but they were accustomed to knock-backs. As Erin was accustomed to knock-backs on their behalf.

'I have a proposition,' he said, and they stared in incomprehension.

'A…a propos…'

'An idea. If you're willing.'

'What's your idea?' They were all looking at him. Charlotte and Bradley. William and Henry.

And Erin.

Mostly Erin. Or maybe it was mostly Erin he was aware of.

'You've seen how quiet Cecil is?' He was talking more to Erin than the twins, aware it was she he had to convince rather than them.

'Yes.'

'Then if I take him to the entrance and get him into position in the parade, would Erin allow you to take him around the arena for me?'

There was an audible intake of breath from every last one of them—including from Matthew himself. Was he mad? Trusting his precious bull to two urchins?

But he looked down into their incredulous faces and he knew that he had nothing to fear at all. Cecil would be as safe as houses. They considered him theirs, and he was as precious to the boys now as their Tigger.

Heaven help anyone or anything that threatened their Cecil!

Bradley was the first to find his voice. Of course.

'You'd trust your beast to these…' He paused, stuck for words, and then found what he was looking for. 'These brats?'

'They're not brats,' Matt said evenly. 'They're my right hand men, and I'd rather trust my bull to these two than to hired hands—as you have your precious horse.' It was impossible to keep the disdain from Matt's voice. Bradley might come from a family who bred champion steeple-chasers, but you'd never catch Bradley doing anything as menial as grooming.

And as for calling his kids brats!

Erin's kids, he reminded himself hastily. Not his. Erin's.

'Matt, you're not serious.' It was Charlotte, putting in her two-bob's worth, but Matt's eyes were on Erin.

'Erin? Is it okay with you?'

Erin thought about it for a whole two seconds flat. For her precious twins, to be given such a trust at the focal point of the most prestigious show in the country....

She met Matt's look head on, and the eyes looking back at him were bright with tears.

'Of course it is,' she managed. 'If you want to, boys.'

'If we want to?' The twins could scarcely breathe for the enormity of what they were being asked. 'You mean....lead him around the ring...all by ourselves?'

'All by yourselves,' Matt said solemnly, still watching the wave of emotion washing over Erin's face. 'If I didn't think you were capable I wouldn't ask it of you. I'll be standing at the pavilion doors, waiting for you to bring him back, but once he's out in the arena he's all yours.'

Charlotte was not impressed! In fact, Charlotte was about as seriously annoyed as Erin had ever seen her.

Bradley had disappeared to take charge of his horse—his lads had done the work but there was no way *he* intended handing over the glory to anyone else. Matt and the twins took themselves off to place Cecil in his parade order, and Erin and Charlotte were left together, to do whatever they wished.

Charlotte didn't wish.

'If I hadn't come in Matt's blasted truck I'd go home now,' she muttered as the last of the menfolk disappeared from view. 'I only wanted to see Matt in the grand parade.'

She did, too, Erin thought as she followed her through the door to the stadium. Matt was a man who stood out in any crowd, and to sit in the stadium and casually let all around her know that there was her fiancé... Well, for Charlotte it was the culmination of twenty years of effort.

Instead of which, she had to content herself with two seven-year-olds leading the bull of her fiancé—and it hardly had the same impact to say; 'Those children are leading my fiancé's bull!'

'I guess you can always watch Bradley,' Erin told her, determined to be good-humoured with the woman. She was feeling so cheerful herself she felt like doing a little jig on the spot. For her twins to be given such responsibility... She tucked her arm into Charlotte's and refused to withdraw it even as Charlotte tugged sharply away.

Maybe she had to be even nicer. 'Hey, Charlotte, I'm sorry for saying what I threatened about your poetry,' she told her. 'You know I'd never really tell anyone—and, in truth, Shanni burned them.'

'We were only teenagers,' Charlotte said, displeased to the core. As well as having to put up with the absence of Matt in the parade, she also had to put up with this disreputable member of the lower orders acting as if she was her friend. Her friend!

Charlotte plumped herself down on a seat and huffed. Not put off in the least, Erin plumped beside her. 'It was just childish stupidity. I'd forgotten all about it,' Charlotte added.

'Bradley hasn't,' Erin told her thoughtfully. 'You must know that. He's always thought you were the ant's pants.'

'There's no need to be coarse!'

'Why have you always refused to go out with him?' Erin said curiously, and got an angry glance for her pains. When Erin still looked an enquiry, Charlotte thrust out her diamond-adorned ring finger, as if that explained all.

'Because Matt and I—'

'Not at fifteen,' Erin told her flatly. 'Or even at twenty-three. If I remember rightly, Matt didn't go out with any-one until he was seventeen, and then it was with Sally McKinley.'

'How on earth do you remember that?'

'I was three years younger than you and Matt,' Erin told her simply. Her eyes twinkled. 'Come to think of it, I still am. But then…well, Matt was school captain and a hunk even then, so whatever he did was the cause of major school gossip. He and Sally—'

'I don't want to hear.'

'No.' Erin chuckled her agreement. She paused, scanning the cattle starting to emerge from the pavilion, but there was still no sign of Cecil and the twins. More to keep her mind off what the twins might or might not be doing, she kept right on probing. 'But I seem to remember that Bradley was good-looking, too. Why would you never go out with him?'

Silence while they both thought back, remembering.

It had been no secret that Bradley had been keen on Charlotte. The poetry had been part of years of secret notes, and Bradley's despair, inexpertly disguised and pounced on with glee by his peers and by those younger than him.

Bradley, in his teens, was a spoiled brat and, as far as the rest of the students were concerned, his passion for Charlotte made him fair game. Especially the impover-ished and scorned younger set to which Erin belonged.

More silence.

Normally Charlotte would simply ignore a question such as Erin had just posed. Normally she would just ignore Erin.

But things weren't normal today. Charlotte's social set weren't here— 'Really, darling, cattle shows, you know. Not our scene!' Her two men were both out of reach and Charlotte had to either sit alone in the stands or pretend to talk politely to Erin.

She could do it. Erin had been grooming bulls for hours, both Cecil and others. She looked like a farm hand—someone the elegant Charlotte would employ. So she could spread her finger so the morning sun just glinted on her diamond, and give the impression that her purpose here was to discuss cattle quality with the staff.

And she was feeling so grumpy with Matt, she might as well tell all…

'I could have had both of them,' she confided, and Erin's eyebrows rose. Respectfully. She was playing along for all she was worth here. She could have been a peasant, shocked to the core by the goings-on of aristocracy, and Charlotte's carefully controlled trill of laughter through the stands meant Erin's ploy was working.

'Oh, not both at once,' she continued. 'But yes, Bradley was certainly keen. He's still keen now. He's asked me to marry him—oh, I've lost count of the times.'

'So why not accept? Why pick on… I mean, why did you choose Matt?' Erin asked respectfully, and once again, Charlotte laughed.

'Are you kidding? There's no choice. Matt's family have had their land forever. His grandfather even had a title!'

Charlotte gave Erin her aristocrat to low life look, meaning with her level of intelligence Erin couldn't possibly understand, but Erin did. There were still people to whom the phrase 'old money' meant something, and Charlotte was certainly one of them.

She chose her words carefully. 'So otherwise, you didn't really mind which one you chose?'

'Of course I did.' Charlotte simpered and waggled her diamond bearing finger some more. 'I'm engaged to Matt, aren't I?'

'Of course.'

'And…'

But Erin was no longer listening.

The twins had emerged from the pavilion doors. They were leading Cecil, and Erin was effectively silenced.

So was Charlotte. She puckered her lips in distaste as the twins proudly and solemnly led their charge around the ring. Erin knew that all Charlotte could think of was, why wasn't Matt leading them?

And Erin was thinking of Matt, too, but in a totally different way. Her gaze never left the faces of her two little boys, and all she could feel was gratitude.

She was so grateful she felt like weeping. Damn, she was weeping!

Below her was the purest of pure bloodstock, being led by the cream of the nation's farmers—and in their midst were her two abandoned and unwanted little boys.

They were all she could see, and she could only see them through a mist of tears. They were totally unsmiling, and solemn as judges—every sliver of concentration bent on leading their charge around the arena with the dignity he deserved.

What a gift!

Erin sat absolutely motionless, with every fibre of her being willing nothing to go wrong. Nothing did, and when the boys had taken Cecil twice around the arena and Matt had come forward to help them tug him back through the great pavilion doors, Erin reached for her handkerchief and blew her nose. Hard.

Charlotte shifted sideways in distaste, but Erin couldn't give a toss.

'Well...' Somehow she managed to find her voice. She rose, and the smile she gave Charlotte was tremulous. 'That's it, then. Are you coming to congratulate them?'

'What, congratulate the twins? You have to be kidding!'

'I meant all of them,' Erin said carefully. 'Matt, too.'

But Charlotte was fed up with a Matthew she hadn't been able to boast about. 'Bradley's not out yet,' she said shortly. 'I'll stay and watch the horses. At least Bradley has the sense to lead his own beast out.'

Sense?

Maybe. It wasn't 'sensible' for Matt to let the twins lead Cecil, Erin thought.

It wasn't sensible in the least.

It was just plain wonderful!

It was a subdued set of twins Erin took back to the farm, and it was a very quiet time Erin had of it for the next few days. It was as if they needed time to absorb what had happened to them. They simply couldn't believe it.

The Grand Parade had been televised. Expecting Matt and Cecil to be in it, Shanni had had the forethought to videotape the program. She and Wendy brought the tape out to the farm and the twins watched themselves on television over and over again.

'It's a miracle,' Wendy said frankly, watching the pair of them. Usually unable to sit still for more than two minutes at a time, the twins had been still for more than half an hour, and Shanni was growing more and more incredulous. 'How on earth have you done it?'

'I haven't done anything,' Erin said, a trace of trouble in her voice which her friends could hardly miss. 'It's Matt who's transformed them. They follow him like two little shadows.'

'And that's a problem?'

'I think it may be.'

'Why?' Wendy probed gently. 'Maybe Matt's just what they need.'

'But it's a temporary arrangement.' Erin shook her head and watched the children for a bit longer. 'I just…worry, I guess. At what will happen when they're moved on, yet again.'

'And how about you?'

'I'm sorry?'

'How about you, Erin Douglas?' Wendy hadn't been Erin's friend for years without being able to read her face like a book, and she didn't like what she was reading now. 'How heart-whole and fancy-free are you? When it's time to move on—will you be able to walk away without a backward glance?'

It was two weeks before Charlotte dropped her bombshell, and those two weeks probably ranked as two of the happiest of the twins' lives. And Erin's.

The farm was one huge playground.

Now that Matt had showed his trust in the twins, they repaid him with absolute loyalty. They kept up their allotted duties as Sadie-replacements until Sadie became tired of limping and took her duties back with relish. They obeyed every spoken and unspoken command the wonderful Matt directed at them. Occasionally even Erin was brought up short by the twins' curt command:

'Will Matt think this is okay?'

And Matt usually did, because Matt, too, was enjoying

himself. The twins and Erin herded his cattle. They helped cut and bale his hay. The climbed his haystacks, they swam in his river, they roamed his farm...

And usually he wasn't far behind them. If Erin took the twins down to the river for a swim, ten to one he'd arrive within the hour—'just to check that things are okay'.

'How can they be anything else?' Erin would demand. 'You have the boys hypnotised. Honestly, Matt, they're starting to love you.'

But he didn't see the problem. Only Erin saw it, and she worried about it.

And she worried about herself, too. This was only for six months, she told herself firmly. This was only until the Home was rebuilt.

And then she had to walk away from here. And leave Matt to Charlotte.

But it wasn't to be for six months.

They'd hardly seen Charlotte since Lassendale. Matt had disappeared a couple of times to visit her for dinner, but Erin and the twins were *persona non grata* with Charlotte—and that was the way they liked it.

So it was with some surprise that they saw her car pull up one morning early after breakfast. Charlotte gave the car door a business-like slam and strode purposefully toward the house.

'Uh, oh,' said William, and Erin thought the same. Matt rose to greet his beloved and the three watched with interest. No passionate hugs here, thought Erin. Matt smiled a welcome, but they didn't even touch.

'Hi, Charlotte? What brings you here?'

'Because I've been longing to see you.' That was what she should have said, Erin thought and with a blinding flash of clarity she also thought, that's what I would have said. Instead, Charlotte said no such thing.

'Because I have such good news,' Charlotte told him, not even bothering to greet Erin and the children. 'Priscilla's has had a cancellation and the church is free at the same time!'

'Priscilla's?'

'You know Priscilla's. The great reception house up in the hills behind town. It used to belong to Sir Reginald Chester and his family but they let it go to ruin. The people who've restored it have done such a fantastic job. It's the best, Matthew, and it's the only thing that's been holding up our wedding as I refuse to hold our reception anywhere but at the best. Mummy agrees. But now it's all set. Four weeks from today. Then two weeks' honeymoon on Norfolk Island and back here as man and wife.'

And she looked at Erin for the first time—and beamed.

Erin flinched.

She couldn't live with this woman, she thought, even if she was welcome. And the thought of playing third party to a newly-wed Matt and Charlotte made her feel ill.

'I... That's great,' she managed. Her eyes moved to Matt who was looking distinctly uncomfortable. 'I'll organise something with Tom. If we can stay for those six weeks, we'll be out before you're back from your honeymoon.'

'You're welcome to stay,' Matt started but Charlotte cut in over him.

'Of course you'll stay until we get back from our honeymoon,' she said sweetly. 'But after that... Matt and I have talked about it. Three adults looking after two children is a bit of overkill—wouldn't you say, Erin?'

'Well—'

'Of course it is. And Matt won't hear of moving the children out until the orphanage is rebuilt.' She tucked her arm in his, society hostess approving her slightly eccentric husband's absurd acts of generosity. 'So after we return, I'll play mother to the boys.' She looked doubtfully at Erin. 'I suppose the Orphanage can find somewhere for you to stay.'

She's acting like I'm an orphan myself, Erin thought wildly. Good grief!

'Erin can stay here,' Matt growled but Erin and Charlotte ignored him.

'You're saying you and Matt wish to be the boys' foster parents?' Erin demanded. She felt sick.

Why, though? She had no right to be. The boys weren't hers.

And if Matt loved them then maybe it'd turn out to be a long-term solution for them. They loved Matt so much, and as long as they stayed out of Charlotte's way...

Which wasn't going to happen, she decided, marshalling her thoughts as the twins looked on in confusion. Charlotte had made not the slightest effort to conceal her dislike of the children. How could the twins possibly be expected to ignore that dislike?

They'd cause trouble the minute Erin left.

'You'd be good for us, wouldn't you?' Charlotte asked them, gimlet-eyed. Dear God, Erin thought. Maybe they would, and the thought of subdued twins was almost worse than the thought of naughty ones.

'I'll have to talk to Tom before I can agree,' she managed. 'Tom's the director of Bay Beach Orphanage. Arrangements like this are up to him.'

In answer, Charlotte gave her lovely, soft, carefully cultivated laugh.

'It's a wonderful offer, Erin. How could Tom refuse?'

How indeed?

CHAPTER TEN

'I'M SORRY that was sprung on you.'

Charlotte hadn't stuck around for long. 'With only four weeks to go I have so much to organise. Goodness, Matt, we haven't even sent out the invitations yet. Mother and I have so much to do.' And with that she was gone.

The twins, not understanding a word of what had been said—they'd formed the habit of tuning out whenever Charlotte was around—had left to do their allotted morning tasks, and Erin was left facing Matt.

She felt sick. What had he said? She gave herself a mental shake, hauling her thoughts together. 'I guess you don't have to be sorry. It's been very generous of you to offer to have us this long, and we now have another six weeks.'

'You can all stay for as long as you want,' he said, more forcibly than he'd intended, and Erin gave him a half hearted smile.

'Matt, you know that's not possible. Six weeks will give us time to find...'

'Erin, I want the twins!'

That startled her. She sat back and looked at him, and for the first time saw the pain and the longing behind his eyes.

Pain? Matt? Matt who'd been so careful for his whole life to keep him existence emotion free? Who was marrying Charlotte as yet another way to keep his world ordered and emotionless.

And yet there was definitely pain. And longing.

166

'You want to keep them?' she asked incredulously and he nodded.

'Yes. Hell, Erin, they're great kids. If I can persuade Charlotte... If I can get her used to them, then I'll adopt them. God knows they deserved better treatment than they've been getting.'

'I look after them,' she said, and got a swift shame-faced smile for her pains.

'Of course you do. I didn't mean to infer that you don't. But you know what Bay Beach is like. Like every local, I've heard their story, and what I didn't know exactly I've heard by asking around. And I think, if Charlotte gets to like them...'

'Do you think she will?'

'They'll be outside with me most of the time.' He gave her a half-hearted grin. 'She knows I want children and this way she won't have to get pregnant to have them. That'll be a bonus.'

A bonus? Was he kidding? Erin thought of the possibility of bearing babies for Matt, and she felt her heart constrict at the thought. There was a wave of almost indescribable longing...

Stop it, Erin, she told herself sharply. There was nothing down that road but pain.

'So you'll have a wife and family with minimum effort,' she managed, and he nodded as if her question was entirely reasonable.

'Yes. I could even enjoy it.'

'You think the boys could, too?'

'I don't see why not?'

'They need a mother.'

'They can get by with just me.'

There. He'd said it. It hung between them, cold and flat,

an expression of what he knew his marriage would be. An expression of all he'd learned the world held.

The twins didn't *need* a mother. He didn't *need* a wife.

Well, he didn't, he thought bleakly, and why the sight of Erin, white-faced and trying desperately to disguise her desperation, should have the power to move him, to make him want to reach out and take her hands in his and hold her...

For comfort, he told himself harshly. For nothing but comfort!

'It won't work, Matt,' Erin said sadly. 'It's a fine offer but the boys need a family.'

'We would be a family.'

'Nope.'

'Erin, you can't keep them forever. You're being selfish.'

'And you're being blind.' She rose, and she felt blind herself. Washed-out and ill. This man was so special, and he was committing himself to a woman who resembled nothing so much as a piece of cold cod fish. And he was committing because Charlotte wouldn't interfere with his life. Because he didn't know what a family could be.

She could show him, she thought wildly. She could teach him.

But her help wasn't being asked for. All she could do was look out for her twins.

'I need to talk to Tom,' she said bleakly. 'I can't make any promises. If Tom says it's okay, then it's none of my business.'

'Let him try.'

'I beg your pardon?'

'You heard what I said?' There were two women and one man seated in the kitchen of Bay Beach Orphanage

Home Number One. The twins were outside with the other kids, and Lori, Erin and Tom were sitting at the kitchen table holding mugs of coffee before them. The mugs were ignored. There was trouble on all of their faces.

Erin had outlined the basic facts. Lori, who'd heard an interesting version of what was happening from Wendy, was wise enough to keep her own counsel, and Tom had reached his own conclusions.

'From what I've heard, Charlotte's not the woman to make the twins happy,' he said. 'But the twins think Matt's great and he can keep them under control. Okay, he's made the offer and it's a good one. We owe it to the boys to see if it'll work.'

'But—'

'I'm not leaving them there indefinitely,' Tom said, raising his hand to silence her. 'Nor am I making other arrangements for you yet, Erin. We've put too much trouble into the boys and seen too much improvement to risk losing all our good work now. What I suggest is that we ask Matt and Charlotte to spend a weekend together before the wedding. With the boys. If, after that, they still want to go ahead with keeping the twins, then we'll assess them as potential foster parents.'

'Tom…'

'It's a gamble,' he said, his wise eyes resting on Erin and seeing things that maybe she didn't even realise she was showing. 'But we'll take it.'

It was a very long shot, Tom thought, and it wasn't entirely the twins' future he was fighting for here. But maybe it was worth the taking.

Erin never found out what means Matt used to persuade Charlotte to spend a weekend of her precious wedding

preparations caring for the twins. All she knew was tha
he had.

'Tom's right. It's sensible,' he told her. 'For us to com
back from our honeymoon and have no idea how to car
for the boys—well, it'll be less of a shock for everyone i
we do it this way.'

'I don't like to leave them,' Erin said doubtfully an
Matt thought suddenly that he knew exactly how she fel
He didn't like her leaving either. But that was emotio
speaking. If it had to be, then this was the best way.

'You know we're capable of looking after the boys.'

'No one's capable if they make up their minds to b
trouble.'

'They behave for me,' Matt told her.

'I know.' But she was still troubled.

And the twins were *not* pleased. 'Why do you have t
go?'

She had her reason all worked out. 'You know Shanni
She's expecting another baby, she's tired and her hus
band's just had an operation. She needs help, and I'v
offered to give her a little holiday.' That much was th
absolute truth. If Erin had to take a break she might a
well make herself useful.

'We don't like it when you go away.'

'You know I had breaks as a House Mother. You cope
then.'

'But we didn't like it,' Henry said mutinously. 'We al
ways get into trouble when you're away.'

Oh, dear!

'You won't get into trouble when you're staying wit
me,' Matt told them, clapping his big hands on their shoul
ders and smiling down at them with a no-nonsense smile
'Charlotte and I can look after you very well.'

'We don't like Charlotte.'

'You hardly know Charlotte.' This was stupid. Arguing with children?

'Erin, where will you be?' William's eyes filled with tears, and Erin's heart clenched. Heck, they'd wrapped themselves around her heart like a hairy worm. She loved them so much—and she had to set them free. This way was right, she told herself fiercely. This way they had a chance of what they needed most in the world. A family.

'I won't be far,' she told them.

'She'll just be around the other side of the bay,' Matt told them, missing Erin's warning glance. She knew it wasn't safe to be specific as to her whereabouts, but he didn't pick it. 'In fact, if we go down to the beach this afternoon and take the binoculars, you'll be able to see Nick and Shanni's house across the sea.'

'Is it near?'

'Near enough for me to come right back on Sunday night,' Erin told them. 'I'll be gone for two sleeps and then I'll be back. So no problems. Please?'

'They'll be fine.' A heavily pregnant Shanni waddled into her friend's bedroom with two cups of hot chocolate and handed one over to her friend. 'Come on, Erin. It's Friday night at nine o'clock and you're worried already. By Sunday you'll be a nervous wreck.'

'And I should be doing this for you.' Erin took her chocolate and grimaced in guilt.

'Nick made it,' Shanni said placidly. 'He's still on sick leave, and Doc Emily says he might as well make himself useful. Light housework is fine, she told him, and you should have seen his face when she said it. Court appearances are out, but ironing's in.'

Erin chuckled, but her heart wasn't in it.

'If only I could be sure Charlotte would look after them.'

'Hey, she's not a monster.'

'She's close!'

'Matt loves her. She must have something going for her.'

'Matt thinks she won't disturb his life. That's why he's marrying her. She's just like his mother.'

'Hmm.' Shanni plonked herself down on Erin's bed and the bed sagged alarmingly. 'Boy, I'm huge,' she said placidly. 'Not disturbing his life, hey? That's not much of a basis for a marriage.'

'It's what he wants.'

'Is it, I wonder?' Shanni asked. 'Or is it just what he thinks he wants?' She wiggled more comfortably onto the bed and let her mug of chocolate rest on her very pregnant bulge. The baby inside her moved and her hot chocolate splashed onto her robe. She ignored it, as if such events were commonplace.

'Nick used to think he liked being a bachelor,' she added contentedly. 'And here he is and he couldn't be happier. Sometimes...well, sometimes men don't know what they want. Sometimes it's up to us women to show them.'

'I sure don't know how.'

'Hmm,' Shanni said again, and the look she cast at her friend was very thoughtful indeed.

It had to be tonight. Damnation! Just when he wanted to spend the night with the twins, he was forced to leave them with Charlotte.

But he had no choice. One of Matt's prize cows was down with her first calf, and she was in all sorts of trouble. At eight Matt rang the vet, and at ten they were both knee deep in trouble.

From dinner time on, Matt didn't see the twins. There

couldn't be a problem with them though, he told himself, as he worked on into the night. Charlotte had decreed that dinner was to be followed by the twins' bedtime. That should be fine. So when finally his calf was successfully born, he headed wearily for the house with only a little guilt weighing him down.

But he couldn't help thinking it would have been better if he'd been able to say goodnight to the twins himself.

And, at first glance, things were just fine.

Charlotte was sitting placidly in the sitting room waiting for him. This was the vision he'd had when he'd asked her to marry him, he thought as he opened the door. A man should come home to this, rather than what he was accustomed to—solitude and take-away pizza.

Charlotte was looking serene and lovely, and the room was looking beautiful to match. Even though the night hardly warranted it, the wind was getting up and she'd lit the fire. The vases were filled with carefully arranged flowers. She'd waxed the furniture, and all his mother's carefully acquired porcelain pieces had been polished.

The room looked just as it had when his mother had been alive, and he paused on the threshold for a moment to savour it.

Order and calm, and two great kids in bed, sleeping soundly.

This was what he'd always known was right, and, as he crossed the room to give Charlotte a swift kiss of appreciation, he thought finally that he'd done the right thing.

But apparently not completely. Charlotte's nose was wrinkling in distaste.

'Phew. Matthew, you smell.'

'Hey, I've washed and taken off my boots,' he told her, offended. This was good, clean cattle smell after all. 'I thought I'd come and find you before I took a shower.'

'Then think again,' she told him calmly. 'Cattle smells in the living room are unacceptable.'

'But we've succeeded in delivering a great little calf.' He was determined to tell her his good news. 'Mum and calf are both well.'

'Matt…'

'Aren't you interested?'

'After you've showered.'

'Fine.'

Only it wasn't fine. He knew instinctively that if Erin was here she'd be excited for him. Sure, the flowers wouldn't be gorgeously arranged—maybe there'd be a bunch of daisies in a jam jar—and the porcelain wouldn't be polished but…

Hell! This was what he wanted—wasn't it?

'I'll just go and check the twins,' he said and her brow snapped down as if he'd just mentioned something else that was distasteful.

'There's no need. They're asleep.'

'You didn't have any trouble with them?'

'Only a stupid argument about them sleeping in the same bed. They're too old to do that. It seems they both wanted to sleep with that disgusting stuffed toy they insist on sharing. I solved the problem by taking it away from them.'

Silence. Then…

'You took away Tigger?' he said cautiously.

'Is that what they call it?' she said, and her voice was indifferent. 'It's revolting. I locked it in the pantry.'

He guessed he could only be thankful she hadn't burned it! 'But they're asleep anyway?'

'Of course.'

Only, of course, they weren't. When he checked, they weren't even in their beds.

*   *   *

'Erin?'

It was midnight. The phone had echoed through Shanni and Nick's home, shrill with urgency, and Nick had answered it on the third ring. He'd listened in appalled silence, and then come to find Erin. Now, standing in the hall in her bare feet, she heard Matt's fear echoing down the line.

'What is it, Matt?'

'Erin, the twins have gone.'

'Gone.' She took a deep breath, fighting down panic as she forced herself to think it through. Erin hadn't survived this long as a House Mother by giving way to hysterics at every scare. 'You mean they've run away.'

'It looks like it.'

'I...okay, Matt.' She took a deep breath. 'There's no problem. You told them I was just around the bay, remember? They'll be walking on the beach somewhere. I'll come.'

'No.'

'N... No?' She really took on board his fear then, and it was vivid and dreadful. It reached her heart, as his statement that the twins had disappeared had not. 'Why not?'

'I've checked. Like you, I thought of the beach first, so I took the farm bike down there straight away. But I went by the river first. Shanni and Nick's house looks miles by beach, but it looks much closer across the water. The twins will have seen that. Erin, the rowing boat's gone, and the tide's running out at full pace. If they took the boat, they'll now be well out to sea.

'They promised they wouldn't use the boat,' Matt muttered. 'They promised.'

Quarter of an hour later, Erin and Matt were in the police launch, headed out into the bay—along with half the

fishing population of Bay Beach. Every boat that wasn't
already out fishing was called into action. Rob McDonald
was taking no chances.

'I want them found, and I want them found fast. If they
realise they're drifting away from land, there's no telling
what they'll do.'

'But they promised,' Matt said again into the night, and
there was quiet desperation behind his words. 'Maybe
we're wrong to be looking out to sea. Maybe they haven't
used the boat. It could have broken away itself. Erin, I
trusted them not to break their word.'

'I think they're in the boat—and I don't think they've
broken their vow. Or—not on their terms.' Erin's voice
was winter-bleak.

'Erin, I heard them promise. I trust them.'

'And you know what I said when they promised?' she
whispered into the night. The boat was slipping out of the
harbour, a flotilla of fishing boats behind them. 'I said:
"While you're living with me you obey my rules." And
then I left them.'

He closed his eyes. 'Erin...'

'It's not your fault,' she said bleakly. 'It's mine. I let
Tom talk me into this, and I might have known it would
end in disaster.'

Dear God...

The sea mist had slipped in over the water. The night
was almost eerie in its stillness. They stood alone in the
bow, each feeling sick with what they might or might not
find before them.

Erin didn't know where Charlotte was. She didn't ask.
Once she'd heard about Tigger's removal, it was maybe
just as well she didn't know.

Dear God... It was a prayer, said over and over again
into the night.

Instinctively, Matt's arm came out and held Erin hard around her waist. For a moment she resisted, but her need for comfort was too great. She let herself be pulled into him, and they stayed that way as the rolling swells of the open sea hit the boat and Rob turned the launch out of the harbour and along the bay toward the tidal outpouring from the river.

Matt and Erin didn't move. They were a man and woman as one. With one prayer...

It was the longest night Erin had ever known.

The flotilla formed a pack. Rob and the most senior of the fishermen worked out a pattern of grid lines based on tides, currents and wind, and each boat was given a course to follow. It was a myriad of criss-crossing lines, with all hands of every boat glued to the guy ropes, and all eyes trying desperately to pierce the fog.

Somewhere in this vast sea were two little boys in a rickety old rowing boat that was never intended to be strong enough to be buffeted by waves like this.

The sea wasn't at its wildest, but it was rough enough to frighten a grown man in an open rowing boat—much less children.

'They don't even have Tigger,' Erin whispered brokenly at one point, and Matt's arm tightened still further. He was trying to instil comfort with every ounce of his being, but at the same time he needed comfort himself.

If only... If only...

He'd been a crazy, blind fool to think this could ever work, he thought. Leaving the twins to Charlotte...

He'd been left with his mother, and he still remembered the coldness. If his father hadn't been there—if he'd had an Erin to run to...

It might have been him in this damned rowing boat, he

thought, and there was something of the lost and lonely child in the look he cast out over the water. Please let the boys be safe, he said to himself and finally out aloud. 'Please…'

'Matt?'

'Mmm.' He could hardly hear. Every ounce of his being was concentrating on trying to pierce the fog. He was willing the boys to appear.

'Whatever happens,' Erin said softly. 'Matt, whatever happens, the boys know that you've loved them. That's meant so much.'

'Not enough,' he managed.

'You're not to blame for this.'

'I am.' He closed his eyes for an instant before pushing them wide to continue searching. 'I am to blame.'

'Why?'

'Because I didn't have the courage to change my life. As I should have done. As I will if I ever have the chance again. Please…'

And finally, just before dawn, they found them.

There was a shout across the water from one of the fishing boats, and then another shout as the boat on the intersecting grid saw what they'd seen.

Immediately every nose of every boat swung into the same point, and Matt and Erin almost fell over the bow in their effort to see.

When they finally did, the fishing boat that had first seen them had seized the rowing boat with a grappling hook and was trying to haul it alongside.

Which was easier said than done. The grappling hook was too short. The rowing boat hit the fishing boat with a sickening crunch, the next wave hit before there was time to lower a man to reach the children, and the fishing boat was forced to pull away. If it hadn't, they ran the risk of crunching the row boat to splinters.

Floodlights played out over the water. The children were crouched low in the boat, clinging to each other in terror.

Rob pulled the police launch in close, but it was so rough he could do nothing. Half filled with water, the old wooden boat was threatening to capsize with every movement. And the twins didn't look up. The men's shouts and the noise of the engines over the roar of the sea was only increasing their terror.

It was too much for Erin. Before anyone could stop her—before anyone could even realise what she intended—she'd grabbed a lifevest and jumped into the water.

One second later, Matt followed.

It took Erin precious minutes to clamber into the rowing boat, and she'd darn near capsized it as she did. But she was born and bred by the sea. The Douglas children had always had boats, mostly home-made by themselves, and there were always too many children in them. She was an expert in keeping old tubs afloat.

And blessedly her self-taught skills didn't let her down. By the time Matt's head appeared, dripping, as he clung to the side, she was holding her two little boys to her as if her life depended on it, and she was able to move backwards to stabilise the boat and let Matt haul himself on board.

And then she had the sense to shift again to the middle. So that once he was safely on board, Matt could take all of them into his arms. It was sandwich squeeze of half-drowned adults and kids, who held each other as if they'd never let each other go again. Forever.

Around them the flotilla of fishermen and police watched with blatant approval and the odd goofy smile. This was the happy ending they'd all wanted so badly.

They should move. They should get the old tub into the lee of the harbour so they could shift the kids out of it.

They should.

But for this moment, no one moved at all. It was as if everyone knew that, right there and then, a family was being forged that would take more power than the sea to split asunder.

CHAPTER ELEVEN

THE children were asleep.

Shocked to the core, they'd been held tight while ropes from the fishing boat tugged them slowly and safely back into the lee of the harbour. Once there, they were transferred to the police launch, William clinging for dear life to Erin, and Henry clinging just as closely to Matt. Then they'd been dried off and brought home.

Charlotte wasn't waiting.

'I said a few unforgivable things to Charlotte,' Matt told Erin briefly, as they put the twins through a warm bath and snuggled them into bed—the same bed—and watched them fall instantly asleep with their precious Tigger between them. 'I don't suppose she'll be back.'

'Oh, Matt, I'm so sorry.'

'Don't be. I've been a fool, and I've been blessed to get out of it as lightly as I have.'

And now, dried and dressed themselves, they were standing in the living room watching the embers of Charlotte's fire die in the grate. The first rays of dawn were breaking over the horizon out to sea.

Erin still hadn't bought herself a decent dressing gown. She was still wearing her huge flannelette welfare handout that made her look about ten years old, and, watching her, Matt thought back to the moment when he'd seen Erin dive from the boat.

Something in him had almost died in that moment. For one awful minute until she surfaced, he'd thought he might lose all of them.

He couldn't bear it. And he couldn't bear to waste another precious minute.

'Marry me, Erin,' he said, and the world held its breath.

She stared. 'M... Marry you?'

'That's what I said.' He took the two short steps to bridge the space between them, and he pulled her to him. Somehow he couldn't bear not to, and as her soft body yielded to his he knew that he could never let her go again.

Dear God, he loved her so much. How had he not known it before? He loved her and loved her and loved her.

But she was pushing him away, and her eyes were troubled. 'Matt, it's just the night. It's shock or something. You love Charlotte.'

'I don't love Charlotte.' He glanced down at the beautifully polished coffee table and there was a diamond ring, lying where she'd tossed it in indignation at what he'd said to her. 'And she doesn't love me,' he continued. 'You see? She's given me back my ring. Not that I want it.'

'So now you...' Erin paused, still troubled. 'You want me to wear it?'

He shook his head at that, absolutely definite. 'No way.' Suddenly his arms were holding her again, and a woman would have to have super powers to resist his hold.

'Not that,' he said. 'Charlotte can have it if she wants it, but you're not wearing her ring. You and Charlotte... you're about as different as two women could be and I was a fool to see it. Erin, I love you. The ring we buy, we buy together, and it'll be a ring full of colour and light. Just like you. Sapphires and rubies and... I don't know. Everything. All the colour you've brought into my life.'

Dear heaven... Somewhere deep inside, Erin's heart was starting to sing.

But not now. Not yet. She couldn't!

'Matt...'

He kissed her lightly on her damp hair, and then, because he could resist no longer, he tilted her chin and kissed her deeply on her mouth. The kiss lasted forever, and was a vow all by itself.

'Yes, love?' he said, and his voice was a husky whisper, filled with passion.

'Matt...' She was trying so hard to make herself say what had to be said. She must! Tonight she'd known. As well as loving this man, she had other loves. 'Matt, I can't leave the twins.'

Was that all that was troubling her? With a shout of triumph, he lifted her high and whirled her above his head. 'The twins? You think I don't love the twins like I'll love my own children? They're part of you, my love. A package deal. It's all or nothing, and I want it all!'

'You...' She was swinging dizzily off her feet. 'You mean you'll adopt the twins?'

'*We'll* adopt the twins,' he said simply, and looking down into his gorgeous, loving eyes she knew at last that he spoke the truth. Here then was her happy ever after ending.

Here was her home.

He set her down on her feet, and his voice became surer. He took her hands in his, and their eyes locked.

'So you'll marry me?' he asked.

Yes, her heart screamed but there were things that needed to be said. It was only fair to warn him.

'Matt, your life will be chaos.'

'I've discovered I love chaos.'

'But you love your mother's lovely things!' She looked

around the room. 'This carpet... The porcelain... There'll be accidents. I know the kids. We won't be able to keep the house to the standards you like.'

The answer to that was easy. He lifted one piece of porcelain—a droopy Romeo and Juliet, for heaven's sake—and let it drop. It hit the grate and smashed into a thousand pieces. Then, as Erin gasped in horror, he grabbed the blackened poker from the fire. Very deliberately he walked across the room and drew in huge letters on the once pristine carpet.

MATT LOVES ERIN!

'Matt!' She was shocked to the core. 'That's vandalism. If you were mine, I'd spank you.'

'Hmm...' His loving eyes mocked a challenge. 'You want to try?'

'Matt McKay!'

'Erin Douglas,' he teased right back. 'Now, will you marry me, or do I have to smash every piece of porcelain in the place before you agree?'

'We'd be much better packing it up as a wedding present for Charlotte and Bradley,' Erin said seriously, and Matt gave a whoop of pure joy.

'Very practical.' She was in his arms again. 'Very sensible. You're my own gorgeous, sensible, crazy, House Mother. My love. My heart. My Erin. Now... Are you going to admit that you'll marry me? Or am I going to have to kiss you senseless, and keep right on kissing you until you finally grow so weak you agree?'

And what was a girl to say to that?

'Yes, please,' she said. 'If only to stop you kissing me senseless.'

'I have news for you,' he told her. 'I intend to do that anyway!'

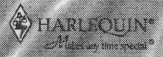

This Mother's Day Give Your Mom A Royal Treat

Win a fabulous one-week vacation in Puerto Rico for you and your mother at the luxurious Inter-Continental San Juan Resort & Casino. The prize includes round trip airfare for two, breakfast daily and a mother and daughter day of beauty at the beachfront hotel's spa.

INTER·CONTINENTAL
San Juan
RESORT & CASINO

Here's all you have to do:

Tell us in 100 words or less how your mother helped with the romance in your life. It may be a story about your engagement, wedding or those boyfriends when you were a teenager or any other romantic advice from your mother. The entry will be judged based on its originality, emotionally compelling nature and sincerity.
See official rules on following page.

Send your entry to:
Mother's Day Contest

In Canada	**In U.S.A.**
P.O. Box 637	P.O. Box 9076
Fort Erie, Ontario	3010 Walden Ave.
L2A 5X3	Buffalo, NY
	14269-9076

Or enter online at www.eHarlequin.com

PRROY

Two ways to enter:

• **Via The Internet:** Log on to the Harlequin romance website (www.eHarlequin.com) anytime beginning 12:01 a.m. E.S.T., January 1, 2002 through 11:59 p.m. E.S.T., April 1, 2002 and follow the directions displayed on-line to enter your name, address (including zip code), e-mail address and in 100 words or fewer, describe how your mother helped with the romance in your life.

• **Via Mail:** Handprint (or type) on an 8 1/2" x 11" plain piece of paper, your name, address (including zip code) and e-mail address (if you ha one), and in 100 words or fewer, describe how your mother helped with the romance in your life. Mail your entry via first-class mail to: Harlequi Mother's Day Contest 2216, (in the U.S.) P.O. Box 9076, Buffalo, NY 14269-9076; (in Canada) P.O. Box 637, Fort Erie, Ontario, Canada L2A 5

For eligibility, entries must be submitted either through a completed Internet transmission or postmarked no later than 11:59 p.m. E.S.T., April 1, 20 (mail-in entries must be received by April 9, 2002). Limit one entry per person, household address and e-mail address. On-line and/or mailed entries received from persons residing in geographic areas in which entry is not permissible will be disqualified.

Entries will be judged by a panel of judges, consisting of members of the Harlequin editorial, marketing and public relations staff using the following crite
  • Originality - 50%
  • Emotional Appeal - 25%
  • Sincerity - 25%

In the event of a tie, duplicate prizes will be awarded. Decisions of the judges are final.

Prize: A 6-night/7-day stay for two at the Inter-Continental San Juan Resort & Casino, including round-trip coach air transportation from gateway airport nearest winner's home (approximate retail value: $4,000). Prize includes breakfast daily and a mother and daughter day of beauty at th beachfront hotel's spa. Prize consists of only those items listed as part of the prize. Prize is valued in U.S. currency.

All entries become the property of Torstar Corp. and will not be returned. No responsibility is assumed for lost, late, illegible, incomplete, inaccura non-delivered or misdirected mail or misdirected e-mail, for technical, hardware or software failures of any kind, lost or unavailable network connections, or failed, incomplete, garbled or delayed computer transmission or any human error which may occur in the receipt or processing of entries in this Contest.

Contest open only to residents of the U.S. (except Colorado) and Canada, who are 18 years of age or older and is void wherever prohibited by all applicable laws and regulations apply. Any litigation within the Province of Quebec respecting the conduct or organization of a publicity contes may be submitted to the Régie des alcools, des courses et des jeux for a ruling. Any litigation respecting the awarding of a prize may be submitt to the Régie des alcools, des courses et des jeux only for the purpose of helping the parties reach a settlement. Employees and immediate famil members of Torstar Corp. and D.L. Blair, Inc., their affiliates, subsidiaries and all other agencies, entities and persons connected with the use, marketing or conduct of this Contest are not eligible to enter. Taxes on prize are the sole responsibility of winner. Acceptance of any prize offered constitutes permission to use winner's name, photograph or other likeness for the purposes of advertising, trade and promotion on behalf of Tors Corp., its affiliates and subsidiaries without further compensation to the winner, unless prohibited by law.

Winner will be determined no later than April 15, 2002 and be notified by mail. Winner will be required to sign and return an Affidavit of Eligibili form within 15 days after winner notification. Non-compliance within that time period may result in disqualification and an alternate winner may be selected. Winner of trip must execute a Release of Liability prior to ticketing and must possess required travel documents (e.g. Passport, photo I where applicable. Travel must be completed within 12 months of selection and is subject to traveling companion completing and returning a Rele of Liability prior to travel; and hotel and flight accommodations availability. Certain restrictions and blackout dates may apply. No substitution of permitted by winner. Torstar Corp. and D.L. Blair, Inc., their parents, affiliates, and subsidiaries are not responsible for errors in printing or electron presentation of Contest, or entries. In the event of printing or other errors which may result in unintended prize values or duplication of prizes, a affected entries shall be null and void. If for any reason the Internet portion of the Contest is not capable of running as planned, including infecti by computer virus, bugs, tampering, unauthorized intervention, fraud, technical failures, or any other causes beyond the control of Torstar Corp. which corrupt or affect the administration, secrecy, fairness, integrity or proper conduct of the Contest, Torstar Corp. reserves the right, at its sole discretion, to disqualify any individual who tampers with the entry process and to cancel, terminate, modify or suspend the Contest or the Interna portion thereof. In the event the Internet portion must be terminated a notice will be posted on the website and all entries received prior to termination will be judged in accordance with these rules. In the event of a dispute regarding an on-line entry, the entry will be deemed submitte by the authorized holder of the e-mail account submitted at the time of entry. Authorized account holder is defined as the natural person who is assigned to an e-mail address by an Internet access provider, on-line service provider or other organization that is responsible for arranging e-mai address for the domain associated with the submitted e-mail address. Torstar Corp. and/or D.L. Blair Inc. assumes no responsibility for any comp injury or damage related to or resulting from accessing and/or downloading any sweepstakes material. Rules are subject to any requirements/ limitations imposed by the FCC. Purchase or acceptance of a product offer does not improve your chances of winning.

For winner's name (available after May 1, 2002), send a self-addressed, stamped envelope to: Harlequin Mother's Day Contest Winners 2216, P.O. Box 4200 Blair, NE 68009-4200 or you may access the www.eHarlequin.com Web site through June 3, 2002.

Contest sponsored by Torstar Corp., P.O. Box 9042, Buffalo, NY 14269-9042.

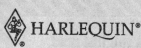

From boardroom...to bride and groom!

A secret romance, a forbidden affair, a thrilling
attraction...where a date in the office diary leads to
an appointment at the altar!

Sometimes a "9 to 5" relationship continues
after hours in these tantalizing office
romances...with a difference!

Look out for some of your favorite

Harlequin Romance®

authors, including:

JESSICA HART: Assignment: Baby
(February 2002, #3688)

BARBARA McMAHON: His Secretary's Secret
(April 2002, #3698)

LEIGH MICHAELS: The Boss's Daughter
(August 2002, #3711)

HARLEQUIN®
Makes any time special ®